IF WE MUST DIE

IF WE MUST DIE

Junius Edwards

HOWARD UNIVERSITY PRESS
Washington, D.C.
1985

Library of Congress Cataloging in Publication Data

Edwards, Junius, 1929–
  If we must die.

Reprint. Originally published: Garden City, N.Y.: Doubleday, 1963. With new introduction.

I. Title	II. Series.		
PS3555.D94I3	1984	813'.54	84–4460
ISBN 0–88258–117-1			

FOR INGER MARIE

Introduction

Ironically, one of the most glaring distinctions of *If We Must Die*, Junius Edwards's only published novel, is that it is an anachronism. It is one of the few novels published by a black writer after the 1950s that may legitimately be given the problematic label of "protest" fiction.

Making such a claim of necessity involves coming to some agreement as to what this label represents, because there are some critics and academicians who would arbitrarily designate nearly all black fiction as protest literature. An article on black novels in the *Encyclopedia of Black America* (McGraw-Hill, 1981, edited by W.A. Low and Virgil A. Clift), for instance, classifies the entire body of black writing from the nineteenth century to the present as either assimilationist, accommodationist, or protest. Those few works designated as accommodationist or assimilationist are more recent and include novels by Ralph Ellison, Willard

Savoy, William Demby, Ann Petry, Chester Himes, and some by James Baldwin. The overwhelming majority of the novels considered, however, are viewed as protest literature. And that category is subdivided into three distinct types: Wrightean, novels in which an oppressed individual or group blindly strikes out at white society; apologetic, novels in which a talented black struggles for success and is thwarted by racism; and militant, novels in which the idea of organized resistance to racial oppression is suggested. In classifying fiction in this manner, the author is obviously assuming a very broad definition of the term *protest;* one that, I would suggest, reduces the term to near meaninglessness.

In its broadest sense, the label protest can be applied to nearly all literature. James Baldwin, in an article on the subject, aptly suggests that the so-called protest novel in the hands of nonblack writers magically becomes the "problem" novel. And the very existence of a protagonist and an antagonist in fictional works suggests that there is some element of protest—that is, a gesture of approval of one entity or idea and disapproval of another. The label is inclusive enough to encompass the works of John Updike or Ann Beattie, who may be said to object to the ennui of middle-class life; or those of Norman Mailer, who proselytizes for a freer, more creative existence and who condemns the numbing constraints of polite, middle-class society; or even those of Harold Robbins, who seems urgently to disapprove of what has been traditionally called a normal sex life. The works of black writers are too easily and too often gratuitously stamped with this trademark because almost all fiction by blacks contains some reference to the inimical social structure in which the authors were nurtured, even when it is not the focus.

Still, unarguably, black American literature has been influenced by the topical experiences, immediate societal imperatives, and general social condition of its practitioners perhaps more than the works of any other American ethnic group. With the possible exception of Jewish literature—which as a whole also vigorously adheres to the concerns and prerequisites of Jewish myth, religion, and sociopolitical history—no other significant body of ethnic American writing so insistently chronicles the sociological plight of its creators and the group they represent. The central reason for this overt strain of parochialism in the writing of black Americans is obvious: most black writers have felt compelled to protest or, in varying degrees, react to both the ongoing bias and discrimination they have encountered in the United States and to white America's simplistic insistence upon perceiving all blacks as variations of a stereotype so fanciful and irrational that it at once comprises the contradictory images of an obsequious, dim-witted, Stepin Fetchit–like figure and the caricatures of the brutish, vengeful buck, which D.W. Griffith so indelibly defined in his portrayal of marauding black rapists in his film *Birth of a Nation.*

Every black American, of course, has had to come to grips with the interconnected problems of adjusting to societal discrimination and to the distorted, often paranoid, perceptual regard of his nonblack fellow citizens. But for black writers of fiction—since they usually are viewed as spokesmen regardless of their intent—the resolution, in so far as it is reflected in their work, presents a formidable puzzle. How to effectively delineate and dramatize the seriousness and dire consequences of the issue? And how to do so while adhering to the established canons of Western literature—the context within which they are working?

One solution is to create a fictional setting in which the central focus is an individual's or a group's struggle for self-fulfillment and recognition. In such works the emphasis is placed on the subjective experience of a protagonist striving to achieve personal fulfillment rather than on the objective obstacles to his struggle. In part, more a reaction to the white majority's stereotypical view of blacks than to the oppressive social structure, fiction of this type accounts for much of the best writing by American blacks. Among those novels that can be loosely placed in this category are Ellison's *Invisible Man*, Baldwin's *Go Tell It on the Mountain*, or more recent works such as James Wright's *The Wig*, Toni Morrison's *The Bluest Eye*, and Alice Walker's *The Color Purple*. These novels do not ignore or diminish concern with the social oppression of blacks, but neither do they make that concern an all-enveloping, dominant theme that distorts the subtle balance among the fictional elements of character, plot, and narrative tone. But, although they may be viewed as imaginative responses to America's failure to recognize the variable human potential of its black citizens, their success by no means suggests that such an approach is a guarantee of estimable fiction. A cursory glance at the earliest published fiction by blacks clearly demonstrates that it is not.

Since it was exceedingly risky, in fact, nearly impossible, in the late nineteenth century and early twentieth century to find a publisher for fiction that directly advocated a change in the social order and attacked the racist attitudes of white Americans, most of these early novels are obvious reactions to the stereotypical assessment of blacks as a group. The authors used stock figures such as the tragic mulatto and the super-sensitive, black intellectual achiever to counteract prevailing stereotypes; the intention was to show that the demeaning characterization of blacks did not apply to all members of the race. Ostensibly appeals for America to live up to its democratic ideals, almost all of these novels dramatized the injustice of applying the exclusionary proscriptions of slavery and Jim Crow to those blacks who were exceptions; rarely were the morally bankrupt policies of legalized human chattel or caste discrimination attacked on a direct, objective level. Still, with the possible exception of James Weldon Johnson's *The Autobiography of an Ex-Colored Man*—initially published anonymously as nonfiction in 1912—none of the novels written by blacks before the 1920s attained any real literary distinction.

Until the modern era of black writing, which had begun with Richard Wright's *Native Son*, fiction more directly concerned with and critical of America's overall discriminatory policies has been even less successful from a literary viewpoint. These novels—in which primary thematic interest was the disclosure of the inhumanity and immorality of slavery and the caste system that took its place—were the inspiration for classifying much of the literary effort of black writers as "protest fiction." And this classification often has been a damning epithet for the fictional work to which it has been applied.

Discussion of the relative merit and effect of protest in black American fiction achieved its most celebrated and, perhaps, revealing airing during the 1960s dialogue between Irving Howe and Ellison. The dispute was ignited by Howe's essay "Black Boys and Native Sons" (*Dissent*, Autumn, 1963), in which he defended Wright's *Native Son* and criticized both Ellison and Baldwin for, among other things, their "modulated" prose.

Howe had been perturbed by Baldwin's criticism of Wright in "Everyone's Protest Novel" (1949) and "Many Thousands Gone" (1951), essays which later appeared in *Notes of a Native Son* (Beacon Press, 1953). In the first critique, Baldwin suggests that Harriet Beecher Stowe's 1852 novel, *Uncle Tom's Cabin,* is the prototype or "cornerstone of American social protest fiction." He then condemns it as a mediocre book, "having in its self-righteous, virtuous sentimentality, much in common with *Little Women.*" Expanding on the effects of sentimentality, one of the key ingredients of most protest fiction, Baldwin continues: "Sentimentality, the ostentatious parading of excessive and spurious emotion, is the mask of dishonesty, the inability to feel; the wet eyes of the sentimentalist betray his aversion to experiences, his fear of life, his arid heart." Baldwin goes on to suggest that Bigger Thomas, Wright's protagonist in *Native Son*, is little more than the reverse portrait of Stowe's obsequious, sexless Uncle Tom. The tragedy of Bigger Thomas, he argues, is not his blackness or even his demeaning experience under the yolk of American racism; it is, instead, his capitulation to a societal image that "denies him life." His misfortune, much as is Uncle Tom's, is that "he admits the possibility of his being sub-human" and accepts the perimeters of existence set forth by the society that has castigated him.

In the latter essay Baldwin cited *Native Son* as the most celebrated fictional treatment of the meaning and consequences of being black in America. While acknowledging that no subsequent work had yet offered a depiction of black life "so indisputably authentic," he argued that the novel had already begun to "bear aspects of a landmark." In effect, he contended that *Native Son* was the ultimate protest novel, a product of a specific time and social climate that, because of black achievement and advancement as well as a more complex and positive assessment of self, was no longer an adequate depiction of the black experience. He also repeated his earlier criticisms of Bigger Thomas and protest literature in general: that in order to demonstrate social injustice and evoke sympathy for its victims the writer is drawn toward sensationalism and the creation of one-dimensional characters. Baldwin's sharpest criticism of *Native Son* was that, by depicting Bigger Thomas as a symbol of the consequences of racism, Wright had created a character who was the very embodiment of white America's myth of the black man.

In response to Baldwin's essays and to Ellison's rejection of naturalism and his views on the "diversity" of the black American experience, Howe came to Wright's defense. He reiterated some of the earlier claims for *Native Son*: that with its appearance "American culture was changed forever"; that it had "assaulted the most cherished of American vanities," among them "the hope that the accumulated injustices of the past would bring no lasting penalties." Howe's assessment extolled the sociological significance of the novel as a warning to white Americans that, far from accepting or forgiving past repression, blacks resent their circumstances, even hate their oppressors, and at any time might seek violent retribution. Although he admitted that the novel has both structural and stylistic problems and that some characters are mere "cartoons," he ultimately lauded its militant outlook and frank handling of the racial problem.

Howe's most remarkable assertion—if for no other reason than its self-righteous condescension—is contained in his general statement about the predicament of black writers. "What, then, was the experience of a man with black skin, what could it be here in this country? How could a Negro put pen to paper, how could he so much as think or breathe, without some impulsion to protest. . . . The 'sociology' of his existence forms a constant pressure on his literary work, and not merely in the way this might be true of any writer, but with a pain and ferocity that nothing could remove."

Howe, then, suggested that protest fiction is the only viable option for black writers. To deny this "pressure" —which "nothing could remove"—to avoid reacting to the burden of societal oppression, is tantamount to denying oneself, one's blackness. And that denial, of course, is exactly what Howe suggested Baldwin and Ellison were guilty of. Despite Howe's good intentions—he no doubt earnestly believed that Bigger Thomas could "shock" Americans enough to change our culture and that the role of the black writer was to induce similar jolts—his blueprint was ultimately as discriminatory and restrictive as those separate facilities that dotted the southern landscape in the not-too-distant past.

In a rebuttal essay, "The World and the Jug" (*The New Leader*, December 9, 1963), Ellison eloquently countered Howe's argument. Alluding to the underlying political thrust of both Howe's attack and Wright's novel, Ellison wrote: "Wright believed in the much abused idea that novels are 'weapons.' . . . I believe that true novels, even when most pessimistic and bitter, arise out of an impulse to celebrate human life and therefore are ritualistic and ceremonial to the core." Then, echoing Baldwin's criticism of the characterization of Bigger, Ellison went on to point out that Wright's protagonist "was presented as a near-subhuman indictment of white oppression" who scarcely hinted at the diversity and richness of black America's life style and concerns. More important, at least with regard to the overall course of black literature, he cited the abject sterility of an aesthetic that would lead black writers to fashion their work only on the models of other black writers.

Besides being an important footnote to the history of contemporary black fiction, the Baldwin–Howe–Ellison dialogue is illuminating with regard to Junius Edwards's novel, for *If We Must Die* undeniably falls into the category of protest fiction.

Edwards's protagonist, Will Harris, is a black veteran of the Korean War who has returned to his small southern hometown. He is primarily interested in living a quiet, inconspicuous life and eventually marrying and raising a family with his financée; as he puts it, "I just want to live like people. Real people." Will's desires are simple. He is not an agitator and wants merely to be treated like a "human being." But as the novel opens, at his mother's insistence, he is preparing to go to the courthouse to register to vote, an act which, in the rural South of the 1950s, represented a grave challenge to the status quo. The gravity of Will's assault on the sanctity of Jim Crow tradition is spelled out in the exchange between Will and his boss, just before he is fired.

> "What did that sign say?" his boss asks,
> "It said all men who want to register . . ."
> "That's right. That's what it said. 'All men.' You think that meant you, boy?"

Within the context of the novel the question is merely rhetorical, for as Edwards illustrates in his description of this single day in Will's life, to be black in the Jim Crow South of the 1950s was, in fact, to accept the limitations of the label "boy." And during the course of the novel, as Will's almost inadvertent transgression leads him further afoul of local authority and custom, the liabilities of that condition are dutifully detailed. *If We Must Die* is ultimately a chronicle of the debasement and humiliation that even the most phlegmatic blacks experienced under a racist, Jim Crow system. As such, it conforms in structure and intent to the basic criterion of protest fiction.

Edwards, however, added a new wrinkle to his novel of protest. Apparently influenced by writers such as Dostoevsky, Kafka, Sartre, Camus, and the existentialism of the 1950s, Edwards, in his novel, dramatizes one of the fundamental precepts of that philosophy: that man is alone, an alien or outsider in a hostile, illogical world over which he has little control. Consequently, Edwards's protagonist is of an entirely different makeup than Wright's Bigger Thomas. While Bigger (after the happenstance encounter that led to Mary Dalton's death) consciously and defiantly challenges the racist society that had victimized him, Will Harris remains a passive victim of racism throughout Edward's novel. Will—like the Algerian clerk in Camus's *The Stranger*, who is driven to murder and finally his own death by seemingly gratuitous, haphazard events—moves in emotional isolation through a series of incidents that are beyond his control. He is little more than a cog in a fatalistic wheel that will conclude with his demise. The novel's ironic ending, in which Will's fate is decided by a black man who is deaf to his pleas, underscores Will's isolation from the outside world as well as his utter defenselessness against its capriciousness. If Bigger Thomas is the embodiment of America's stereotype of the black man as the violent brute, as Baldwin suggested, then Will Harris is a symbol of the black man as an impotent cipher. Every decision that Will makes, every action he takes in the novel is prompted from outside himself—by his mother or fiancée or the local whites. Will's day-to-day routine and livelihood, his very existence (even his death), are dictated by the whims of those around him.

In one sense, Edwards's assimilation of aspects of the existential viewpoint and his rather extreme portrait of Will as a black man overwhelmed by ennui and passivity heighten the novel's overall depiction of the insanity of racism. With Will Harris, Edwards created a black character whose attitude reflects an ontological angst more commonly found in European fiction, and through Will's experience the horror and irrational conceit of American racism are graphically depicted. And the novel's somber, matter-of-fact tone complements this unsettling picture because it ultimately conveys the impression that the societal madness that is inflicted on Will is in no way extraordinary. The understated irony of the fact that Will's ordeal is simply an instance of business-as-usual in the rural South of the 1950s makes *If We Must Die* an even more damning depiction of man's inhumanity to his fellow man.

The disquieting moral message of this short novel notwithstanding, Edwards, like many of the writers who had previously ventured into protest fiction (or, for that matter, many of the European writers who delved into existential fiction with its underlying philosophical and moral themes), fell victim to one of the pitfalls of the genre. Finally, Will Harris's character strains credibility; his apathy verges on caricature, as do the exaggerated simple-mindedness and brutishness of some of the minor characters in the novel. Moreover, in heightening and dramatizing the encounter between Will and the racist environment in which he functions, Edwards allowed the element of sentimentality (which Baldwin correctly designated as the foremost nemesis of protest novels) to assume too great a role in the novel. The extended near-castration scene becomes effusively maudlin.

If We Must Die, however, stands as a significant example of the black writer's continuing effort to extend the perspective from which his experience is viewed in literature. While Junius Edwards's novel harks back to fiction written as early as *Uncle Tom's Cabin* and *Clotelle, The President's Daughter,* (William Wells Brown, 1853) it also incorporates the precepts of contemporary existentialists. And, despite its flaws, it remains a graphic record of the gratuitous and, therefore, even more pernicious consequences of racism.

Mel Watkins
1983

If we must die, let it not be like hogs . . .

CLAUDE MCKAY

Chapter

One

It was six o'clock. Will Harris knew without looking at the clock. He reached for the clock on his night table and pushed the alarm. He didn't want it to ring at six-thirty and wake Mom sleeping in her room. Will had been awake since five. He had stayed in bed and watched the gray chase the dark and, finally, the sun chase the gray. It wasn't time to get up. He had plenty of time. He swung his long legs out of bed and smiled when his feet touched the tickling warmth of the pine. He stood, and stretched. He had plenty of time, but he wanted to be ready.

He had shined his shoes last night and brushed his blue suit good. It did not need pressing. Mom had made

1

sure of that, as she had made sure that he had a newly ironed white shirt. He had read until ten o'clock and then he had taken Mom's advice to go to bed.

He could not sleep. Mom was still up and she heard him moving in bed. She came to his door.

"Come in, Mom."

"Can't sleep, son?"

"No."

She didn't switch on the light. She came to his bed and sat on it just as she had done through the years when he was a little boy.

"Come to tuck me in, Mom?"

She laughed. He liked to hear Mom laugh. Her laugh was deep and real and no matter how he felt her laugh always did something for him.

"You should sleep," Mom said. "You need it."

"I wish I could."

"Are you worried?"

"A little."

"I know how it is. I'm worried too."

"Do you think it's any use, Mom?"

"Yes," she said quickly. "Yes, I know it is."

"I know, Mom. I know it is. It's just that sometimes, well, sometimes I . . ."

"I know, son. I know." She stood. "It'll be all right. Now, you try and go to sleep. You'll need sleep so you can be ready."

They had said good night and he had thought about it all for a long time, until he fell asleep. He hadn't slept well. He woke up three times and when he woke at five he stayed awake.

Now, he went to the bathroom in his bare feet so he wouldn't wake Mom. After he had washed, he tiptoed back to his room and got dressed. He did not put on his shoes. He went to his bookcase and took out *The Story of the Declaration of Independence* and read.

He read until Mom called him to breakfast. It was seven-thirty. He put on his shoes and went to the kitchen.

"Morning, Mom."

She was putting hot biscuits on the table.

"Morning, son."

She turned around and saw him. She smiled.

"My, you look fine," she said. "Just fine."

"Thanks, Mom."

"How long you been up?"

"Quite a while."

"Reading?"

"Yes."

He sat down.

"Sleep good?"

"Fine."

When Mom had called him in to eat, he had been all set to drink a cup of coffee and tell her he wasn't hungry, but her bacon smelled so good and it was so crisp, the way he liked it, he just dug right in.

"I'm so proud of you, son."

What could he say to that when it came from Mom and with that special sound in her voice?

He attacked that second strip of bacon.

3

He could never bring himself to say anything when Mom said that to him, not even thank you, because to him thank you wasn't enough. All he could do was smile.

Mom said that only on special occasions in his life. She said it when he graduated from grammar school and high school, when he came home from Korea, and now.

Will turned twenty-one while he was still in Korea. His birthday present was a letter from Mom. She said she considered him a man when he put on the uniform and fighting in Korea made him more a man and being twenty-one confirmed it. She said that now, since he was twenty-one, he had come to the responsibilities of manhood and that he was old enough to vote.

Will Harris knew how Mom felt about voting. He knew, too, that voting was not such a big thing to some people, but to Mom it was something very special. It had always been. As long as he could remember she had been trying to make herself eligible to vote and all the time she had pounded it into Will how important it was. He didn't know how right she was until after he was in the Army and they told him the same thing, but in a different way. He didn't like military life, but he had to admit the Army taught him more about citizenship and made him think more about it than he had ever done before he became a soldier.

He remembered when election time came while he was still in the Army. The Army told all soldiers who came from states that accepted absentee votes that they were eligible to vote and urged them to send for those ballots and vote. Will sent for a ballot and waited excitedly. It would be his first vote.

Pretty soon those long, official-looking envelopes started to come and it was time to vote. Will knew how some fellows soldiers *looked* like they felt, voting for the first time. He didn't know *how* they felt because he wasn't one of the lucky ones who received ballots. He didn't know what happened. He had sent his request for a ballot. All he knew was that a few soldiers did not get that official-looking envelope and he was one of the few. At first he thought it would come later, but as time passed he realized that it would not come. So many had sent for them, maybe they just couldn't send them to everyone. Red tape. Anyway, he knew he wouldn't miss out next time because he would be out of the Army and nothing in the world was going to keep him from going down and registering and voting.

He didn't tell Mom about sending for the absentee ballot. He had planned to tell her after he had voted. Surprise her. Now he was glad he hadn't told her. After he got out of the Army and went back home, he told her he was going to register and vote in the next election.

Mom told him voting would be easy. She knew that even though she had never voted. The hard thing, she said, was to get registered. The whole thing, registering and voting, she said, was very easy in some states, but not in their state. That was why Mom never made it. It was not easy. Mom wasn't dumb, but they always had some pretty tough questions to be answered when she

5

went down to register. There was always one that stumped her.

Will studied for two years after he was out of the Army. Mom helped him. She helped him by steadily asking him questions that might come. She asked him any time, anyplace. They asked all the people they could find who had ever been down to try to register to tell them what questions they were asked and they wrote them all down and Will learned the answers to them. He got books about the state government, federal government, history, and an almanac, and he studied them all. He also studied newspapers, periodicals, pamphlets from the state capitol, and anything else he could get his hands on. He even studied the Constitution of the United States and his state's constitution.

Then, to top all that, Mom went down to see a lawyer and had their house put in Will's name so he could be even better qualified to vote as a property owner.

Will thought of himself as a funny sort of eater. Most people eat their cereal first and then bacon and eggs. Not Will. He couldn't do that. He always ate two slices of bacon first and then two slices of toast or two biscuits with two eggs, sunny side up, lots of pepper (Mom always said it was too much pepper), little jam and butter (Mom always said it was too little butter). After that, he would eat his cereal before lingering over that last crisp of bacon. Then he would take a cigarette and drink his coffee, fast.

That's the way he ate that morning. He wasn't a bit nervous. Mom was. He could tell Mom was nervous. She didn't eat at all. She just sat there, silent, over a cup of black coffee.

They sat at the breakfast table in silence until Will put out his cigarette.

"You got your birth certificate?"

"Yes."

"Deed to the house?"

"Yes."

"Discharge papers?"

"Yes, Mom."

"High school diploma?"

"Yes, Mom. I have everything."

"Don't be nervous, son."

"I'm not, Mom."

"Remember. Go in there and sit till they call you in, now."

"Yes, Mom."

"No matter how long you have to wait."

"Okay."

"Even if they take other people before you who came in after you."

"Don't worry, Mom."

"No matter how hot you get in there, don't you take off your jacket."

"I won't, Mom."

"Don't forget, now, no matter how good you know the answer, take it slow. Don't give them too fast."

"All right, Mom."

"And son. I don't think you better take along any books to read while you wait. And don't buy a newspaper,

7

neither. I don't think it's a good idea to let them see you reading. They might count it against you."

Mom sure is nervous, thought Will.

"And smoking, son. I . . ."

"I'll hold up from smoking while I'm waiting, Mom."

"That's good, son. That's good. Now, don't forget to . . ."

Yes, Mom was nervous. She went on reminding him about things that he had spent two years learning. It was Mom's way. He just let her go on and she was still telling him things to remember when he went out the front door.

She followed him out.

"Son. I want you to remember, no matter what happens down there today. I'm proud of you. Real proud."

Will kissed her forehead.

He held her shoulders and smiled.

People are sort of funny-acting things, Will thought, they really are. But no matter how funny they act sometimes, most people are all right. Every family in his block knew what he was going to do that day and as he walked down to the bus stop, they waved and smiled. Even people with whom he had never had a word. Some came and shook his hand and smiled up to him. It was like when he came home from Korea.

Will felt pretty good when he got on the bus. He went on back to that big, wide seat in the back of the bus. It was a hot day, anyway, and sitting over the motor made it even hotter back there so he took off his jacket. He sweated easy. He didn't want to be all sweated up when he got down to the courthouse.

When he got off the bus he still had two blocks to walk, so he decided to smoke a cigarette. He liked cigarettes. Mom said he smoked too much, but he kept it up. It was one reason why he didn't like to see double-feature movies. He just couldn't sit that long without a smoke.

He hadn't finished his smoke by the time he got to the courthouse so he stood outside and smoked and then he put on his jacket and straightened his tie and went on up to the second floor.

There was a sign there that told him what to do. He was to go into the waiting room and sit there until he was called in to register. He opened the door to the waiting room and went in. The room was empty. It made him glad. Maybe he wouldn't have to wait long. He closed the door and looked around the room. He didn't know when it was swept last. It had one window over to his left and if it hadn't been opened he didn't know whether the sun would have gotten in through those dirty windowpanes or not. At his right there were two benches. He sat down on the back bench.

He had just finished a cigarette downstairs, but he hadn't been sitting there ten minutes before he felt the urge. All those cigarette butts on the floor don't help, he thought. He looked out the window. There was nothing to see out there. He wondered how long he would have to sit and wait.

He sat there for an hour. During that time, four men came in. He noticed that when the first man came in he didn't bother about the sign and the benches. He just walked right on in the inner office and when he came out he put something in his pocket. Will knew the man had registered. When the first man came and went right on in like that, Will was surprised. By the time the second, third, and fourth men came and did the same thing Will wanted to forget that sign and walk on in and get registered, too, so he could get out of there and have a smoke.

No.

He remembered Mom's words. He sat there. He waited. Waited . . .

Pretty soon, three men came in. The first man was little and he had a smile that Will thought was bigger than the man himself; the kind of smile that made Will feel good from seeing it. The two men who followed him weren't smiling so big. One had a camera. It was easy for Will to see that it was a press camera. The other man had a pencil and pad.

"You all stand over by the door," the man with the camera said, "like you was being interviewed."

The little man and the man with the pencil and pad went over to the door to the inner office and the man with the camera told them how he wanted them to pose and then he took two pictures.

Will sat there and watched them. As he watched them, he had the idea that he had seen the little man before. They had all gone into the inner office when Will remembered. A few days ago, he had seen the little man's picture in the newspaper. The man had just gotten his citizenship papers. The story told how the little man had, a few years ago, escaped from one of the Iron Curtain countries and come to America to live. It told how he had been shot while escaping. Will wondered whether the little man had been shot with a burp gun, the way he had been shot over in Korea. Seeing the little man made Will feel kind of close to him. It must be because both of us have been wounded by communists, thought Will.

The door opened and the man with the camera backed out. His camera was up to his face as he took two more pictures.

"One more with the registrar," he said. He took a picture while the little man and the registrar shook hands.

"How you feel now that you all registered and ready to vote like all other Americans?" the man with the pencil and pad asked.

Will listened and watched.

The little man smiled and Will thought he was searching for words.

"I cannot, how do you say, describe, yes. Describe. I cannot describe the feeling. Not with, not with the words. I got the papers, yes. Yes. I got the papers. Yes. But when I come down here today. Down here to the courthouse to register to vote, it make me feel more like the citizen than when I got the papers. When I got the papers, I knew I was a citizen. I'm so happy. I'm so proud. I'm American. Just like you. Just like you all. I'm American. I tell myself all the time. I'm American. Yes, I do. I hear myself speak and I don't hear myself speak American, but that's all right. That's all right. I learn. Every day, I learn the English."

"You doing fine with English," the photographer said. "Fact is, you talk almost good as us."

"Thank you. Thank you. I don't worry about the speech so much. I learn. I just want to do my, how do you say, duty. Yes, duty. I want to do my duty as a citizen. That's what I want to do. My duty. I could never do my duty as I saw it in the old country. I had to do what they say. But, here? It's America. America. Government here, they don't tell you where to live, how to live, and what to do. And you know why? Because the government is you and me. Me, too. Me, too. America means freedom. Today I come down here to do the biggest thing that any American can do, register and vote."

The man spoke slowly and Will was sure that the reporter was able to get everything written down.

"And do you care to tell us how you're going to vote?" the reporter asked.

"In America, nobody stops you from voting. Nobody tells you how to vote. You don't have to day, I mean, to say, to nobody who you vote for. Nobody. I like that about America. You don't have to be born here to be a citizen and vote and enjoy the freedom. I come here election day and I vote. I vote the way I want to vote. Nobody gets angry. Nobody tells me how. I do it the way I want to do it. I know for sure I am American."

Will watched the three men go on out the door. That

smile was as big as ever on the little man's face. He was so proud to be an American citizen. That little man and his big smile sure made Will feel good.

It made Will smile too.

Chapter

Two

Will Harris sat on the bench in the waiting room for another hour. His pride was not the only thing that hurt. He wanted them to call him in and get him registered so he could get out of there. Twice, he started to go into the inner office and tell them, but he thought better of it. He had counted ninety-six cigarette butts on the floor when a fat man came out of the office and spoke to him.

"What you want, boy?"

Will Harris got to his feet.

"I came to register."

"Oh, you did, did you?"

"Yes, sir."

The fat man stared at Will for a second and then turned his back to him.

As he turned his back, he said, "Come on in here."

Will went in.

It was a little office and dirty, but not so dirty as the waiting room. There were no cigarette butts on the floor here. Instead, there was paper. It looked like candy wrappers to Will. There were two desks jammed in there and a bony little man sat at one of them, his head down, his fingers fumbling with some papers. The fat man went around the empty desk and pulled up a chair. The bony man did not look up.

Will stood in front of the empty desk and watched the fat man sit down behind it. The fat man swung his chair around until he faced the little man.

"Charlie," he said.

"Yeah, Sam," Charlie said, not looking up from his work.

"Charlie. This boy here says he come to register."

"You sure? You sure that's what he said, Sam?" Still not looking up. "You sure? You better ask him again."

"I'm sure, Charlie."

"You better be sure, Sam."

"All right, Charlie. All right. I'll ask him again," the fat man said. He looked up at Will. "Boy. What you come here for?"

"I came to register."

The fat man stared up at him. He didn't say anything. He just stared, his lips a thin line, his eyes wide open. His left hand searched behind him and came up with a handkerchief. He raised his left arm and mopped his face with the handkerchief, his eyes still on Will.

The odor from under his sweat-soaked arm made Will step back. Will held his breath until the fat man finished mopping his face. The fat man put his handkerchief away. He pulled a desk drawer open and then he took his eyes off Will. He reached in the desk drawer and took out a bar of candy. He took the wrapper off the candy and threw the wrapper on the floor at Will's feet. He looked at Will and ate the candy.

Will stood there and tried to keep his face straight. He kept telling himself: I'll take anything. I'll take anything. I'll take anything to get it done.

The fat man kept his eyes on Will and finished the candy. He took out his handkerchief and wiped his mouth. He grinned.

Will held his breath.

The fat man put his handkerchief back.

Will breathed again.

"Charlie."

"Yeah, Sam."

"He says he come to register."

"Sam, are you sure?"

"Pretty sure, Charlie."

"Well, explain to him what it's about." The bony man still had not looked up.

"All right, Charlie," Sam said and looked up at Will. "Boy. When folks come here, they intend to vote, so they register first."

"That's what I want to do," Will said.

"What's that? Say that again."

I'll take anything, Will thought.

"That's what I want to do. Register and vote."

The fat man turned his head to the bony man.

"Charlie."

"Yeah, Sam."

"He says . . . Charlie, this boy says that he wants to register and vote."

The bony man looked up from his desk for the first time. He looked at Sam, then both of them looked at Will.

Will looked from one of them to the other, one to the other. It was hot and he wanted to sit down. Anything. I'll take anything. I'll take anything. Anything, thought Will.

The man called Charlie turned back to his work and Sam swung his chair around until he faced Will.

"You got a job?" he asked.

"Yes, sir."

"Boy, you know what you're doing?"

"Yes, sir."

"All right," Sam said. "All right."

Just then, Will heard the door open behind him and someone came in. It was a man.

"How, you all? How about registering?"

Sam smiled. Charlie looked up and smiled.

"Take care of you right away," Sam said, and then to Will, "Boy. Wait outside."

As Will went out he heard Sam's voice: "Take a seat.

Take a seat. Have you fixed up in a little while. Now, what's your name?"

"Thanks," the man said, and Will heard the scrape of a chair.

Will closed the door and went back to his bench.

Anything. Anything. Anything. Anything. Anything. Anything. I'll take it all. All.

Pretty soon the man came out. Sam came out behind him and he called Will and told him to come in. When Will went in and stood before the desk, Sam told him he wanted to see his papers: Discharge, high school diploma, birth certificate, Social Security card, and some other papers. Will had them all. He felt good when he handed them to Sam.

"You belong to any organization?"

"No, sir."

"Pretty sure about that?"

"Yes, sir."

"You ever heard of the Fifteenth Amendment?"

"Yes, sir."

"What does that one say?"

"It's the one that says all citizens can vote."

"You like that, don't you, boy? Don't you?"

"Yes, sir. I like them all."

Sam's eyes got big. He slammed his right fist down on his desk top. "I didn't ask you that. I asked you if you liked the Fifteenth Amendment. Now, if you can't answer my questions . . ."

"I like it," Will put in, and watched Sam catch his breath.

Sam sat there looking up at Will. He opened and closed his desk-pounding fist. His mouth hung open.

"Charlie."

"Yeah, Sam." Not looking up.

"You hear that?" Looking wide-eyed at Will. "You hear that?"

"I heard it, Sam."

Will had to work to keep his face straight.

"Boy," Sam said. "You born in this town?"

You got my birth certificate right there in front of you. "Yes, sir."

"You happy here?"

"Yes, sir."

"You got nothing against the way things go around here?"

"No, sir."

"Can you read?"

"Yes, sir."

"Are you smart?"

"No, sir."

"Where you get that suit?"

"New York."

"New York?" Sam asked, and looked over at Charlie. Charlie's head was still down. Sam looked back to Will.

"Yes, sir."

"Boy, what you doing there?"

"I got out of the Army there."

"You believe in what them folks do in New York?"

"I don't know what you mean."

"You know what I mean. Boy, you know good and

well what I mean. You know how folks carry on in New York. You believe in that?"

Will knew what answer Sam wanted.

"No, sir," he said.

"You pretty sure about that?"

"Yes, sir."

"What year did they make the Fifteenth Amendment?"

No matter how good you know the answer, take it slow, don't give them too fast. Mom's words rang in Will's ears.

". . . Eighteen . . . seventy. Eighteen-seventy," said Will.

"Boy, what year is this, now?"

"This is nineteen . . ."

Sam cut him off with: "Name a signer of the Declaration of Independence who became President."

". . . John Adams."

"Boy, what did you say?" Sam's eyes were wide again.

Will thought. Then he said, "John Adams."

Sam's eyes got wider. He looked to Charlie and spoke to a bowed head. "Now, too much is too much." Then he turned back to Will.

He didn't say anything to Will. He narrowed his eyes first, then spoke.

"Boy. Did you say *just* John Adams?"

How stupid can I get, Will asked himself.

"Mr. John Adams," he said.

"That's more like it," Sam smiled. "Now, why do you want to vote?"

"I want to vote because it is my duty as an American citizen to vote."

"Hah," Sam said real loud, and pushed back from his desk and turned to the bony man.

"Charlie."

"Yeah, Sam."

"Hear that?"

"I heard, Sam."

Sam leaned back in his chair, keeping his eyes on Charlie. He locked his hands across his round stomach and sat there.

"Charlie."

"Yeah, Sam."

"Think you and Elnora be coming over tonight?"

"Don't know, Sam," said the bony man, not looking up. "You know Elnora."

"Well, you welcome if you can."

"Don't know, Sam."

"You ought to, if you can. Drop on in, if you can. Come on over and we'll split a corn."

The bony man looked up.

"Now, that's different, Sam."

"Thought it would be."

"Can't turn down corn, if it's good."

"You know my corn."

"Sure do. I'll drag Elnora, if I have to."

The bony man went back to work.

Sam turned his chair around to his desk. He opened a desk drawer and took out a package of cigarettes. He tore it open and put a cigarette in his mouth. He looked up at Will, then he lit the cigarette and took a long drag and then he blew the smoke, very slowly, up toward Will's face.

The smoke floated up toward Will's face. It came up in front of his eyes and nose and hung there, then it danced and played around his face and disappeared.

Will didn't move, but he was glad he hadn't been asked to sit down.

Anything. Anything.

"You have a car?"

"No, sir."

"Don't you have a job?"

"Yes, sir."

"You like that job?"

"Yes, sir."

"You like it, but you don't want it."

Will put his hand up to his mouth and coughed from the smoke.

"What do you mean?" Will asked.

"Don't get smart, boy," said Sam, wide-eyed. "I'm asking the questions here. You understand that?"

"Yes, sir."

"All right. All right. Be sure you do."

"I understand it."

"You a communist?"

"No, sir."

"What party do you want to vote for?"

"I wouldn't go by parties. I'd read about the men and vote for a man, not a party."

"Hah," said Sam and looked over at Charlie's bowed head. "Hah," he said again, and turned back to Will.

"Boy, you pretty sure you can read?"

"Yes, sir."

"All right. All right. We'll see about that." Sam took a book out of his desk and flipped some pages. He gave the book to Will.

"Read that loud," he said.

"Yes, sir," Will said, and began, "'When in the Course of human events it becomes necessary for one people to dissolve the political bands which have connected them with another, and to assume among the powers of the earth, the separate and equal station to which the Laws of Nature and of Nature's God entitle them, a decent respect to the opinions of mankind requires that they should declare the causes which impel them to the separation.'"

Will cleared his throat and read on. He tried to be distinct with each syllable. He didn't need the book. He could have recited the whole thing without the book.

"'We hold these truths to be self-evident, that all men are created equal, that they—'"

"Wait a minute, boy," Sam said. "Wait a minute. You believe that? You believe that about 'created equal'?"

"Yes, sir," Will said, knowing that was the wrong answer.

"You really believe that?"

"Yes, sir." Will couldn't make himself say the answer Sam wanted to hear.

Sam stuck out his right hand and Will put the book in it. Then Sam turned to the other man.

"Charlie."

"Yeah, Sam."

"Charlie, did you hear that?"

"What was it, Sam?"

"This boy, here, Charlie. He says he really believes it."

"Believes what, Sam? What you talking about?"

"This boy, here. Believes that all men are equal, like it says in the Declaration."

"Now, Sam. Now, you know that's not right. You know good and well that's not right. You heard him wrong. Ask him again, Sam. Ask him again, will you?"

"I didn't hear him wrong, Charlie," said Sam and turned to Will. "Did I, boy? Did I hear you wrong?"

"No, sir."

"I didn't hear you wrong?"

"No, sir."

Sam turned to Charlie.

"Charlie."

"Yeah, Sam."

"It's just like I told you. I heard right."

The man called Charlie looked up from his desk and at the man called Sam. Then they looked at Will. For a full minute Will just looked from one to the other, one to the other.

"Charlie."

"Yeah, Sam."

"Charlie. You think this boy trying to be smart?"

"Sam. I think he might be. Just might be. He looks like one of them that don't know his place."

Sam narrowed his eyes.

"Boy," he said. "You know your place?"

"I don't know what you mean."

"Boy, you know good and well what I mean."

"What do you mean?"

"Boy, who's . . ." He leaned forward, on his desk. "Boy. Just who's asking questions, here?"

"You are. Sir."

"Charlie. You think he really is trying to be smart?"

"Sam. I think you better ask him."

"Boy."

"Yes, sir."

"Boy. You trying to be smart with me?"

"No, sir."

"Sam."

"Yeah, Charlie."

"Sam. Ask him if he thinks he's good as you and me."

"Now, Charlie. Now, you heard what he said about the Declaration."

"Ask anyway, Sam."

"All right," Sam said. "Boy. You think you good as me and Mister Charlie?"

What the heck, thought Will. Give them the answer they want to hear.

"No, sir," Will said.

They smiled and Charlie turned away.

Will wanted to take off his jacket. It was hot and he felt a drop of sweat roll down his right side. He pressed his right arm against his side to wipe out the sweat. He thought he had it, but it rolled again and he felt another drop come behind that one. He pressed his arm in again. It was no use. He gave it up.

"How many states make up this country?"

". . . Fifty."

"How many stars did the first flag have?"

". . . Thirteen."

"What's the name of the mayor of this town?"

". . . Mr. Roger Phillip Thornedyke Jones."

"Spell Thornedyke."

". . . Capital T-h-o-r-n-e-d-y-k-e, Thornedyke."

"How long has he been Mayor?"

". . . Ten years." Too long, thought Will.

"Who was the biggest hero in the War Between the States?"

". . . General Robert E. Lee."

"What does that *E* stand for?"

". . . Edward."

"Think you pretty smart, don't you?"

"No, sir."

"Well, boy, you been giving these answers too slow. I want them fast. Understand? Fast."

"Yes, sir."

"What's your favorite song?"

"'Dixie,'" Will said, and prayed Sam would not ask him to sing it.

"Do you like your job?"

"Yes, sir."

"What was the last state into the forty-eight?"

"Arizona."

"What year?"

"1912."

"There was another state in 1912."

"New Mexico, but it came in January and Arizona came in February."

"You think you smart, don't you?"

"No, sir."

"Don't you think you smart? Don't you?"

"No, sir."

"Oh, yes, you do, boy."

Will said nothing.

"Boy, you make good money on your job?"

"I make enough."

"Oh. Oh, you're not satisfied with it?"

"Yes, sir. I am."

"You don't act like it, boy. You know that? You don't act like it."

"What do you mean?"

"You getting smart again, boy. Just who's asking questions here?"

"You are."

"That's right. That's right."

The bony man made a noise with his lips and slammed his pencil down on his desk. He looked at Will, then at Sam.

"Sam," he said. "Sam, you having trouble with that boy? Don't you let that boy give you no trouble, now, Sam. Don't you do it."

"Charlie," Sam said. "Now, Charlie, you know better

than that. You know better. This boy here know better than that, too."

"You sure about that, Sam? You sure?"

"I better be sure, if this boy here knows what's good for him."

"Does he know, Sam?"

"Do you know, boy?" Sam asked Will.

"Yes, sir."

Charlie turned back to his work.

"Boy," Sam said. "You sure you're not a member of any organization?"

"Yes, sir. I'm sure."

Sam gathered up all Will's papers and he stacked them very neatly and placed them in the center of his desk. He took the cigarette out of his mouth and put it out in the full ash tray. He picked up Will's papers and gave them to him.

"You've been in the Army. That right?"

"Yes, sir."

"You served two years. That right?"

"Yes, sir."

"You have to do six years in the Reserve. That right?"

"Yes, sir."

"You're in the Reserve, now. That right?"

"Yes, sir."

"You lied to me here, today. That right?"

"No, sir."

"Oh, yes, you did, boy. Oh, yes, you did. You told me you wasn't in any organization. That right?"

"Yes, sir."

"Then, you lied, boy. You lied to me because you're in the Army Reserve. That right?"

"Yes, sir. I'm in the Reserve, but I didn't think you meant that. I'm just in it and I don't have to go to meetings or anything like that. I thought you meant some kind of civilian organization."

"When you said you wasn't in an organization, that was a lie. Now, wasn't it, boy?"

He had Will there. When Sam had asked him about organizations the first thing to pop in Will's mind had been the communists, or something like them.

"Now, wasn't it a lie?"

"No, sir."

Sam narrowed his eyes.

Will went on.

"No, sir, it wasn't a lie. There's nothing wrong with the Army Reserve. Everybody has to be in it. I'm not in it because I want to be in it."

"I know there's nothing wrong with it," Sam said. "Point is, you lied to me here today."

"I didn't lie. I just didn't understand the question," Will said.

"You understood the question, boy. You understood good and well, and you lied to me. Now, wasn't it a lie?"

"No, sir."

"Boy. You going to stand right there in front of me, big as anything and tell me it wasn't a lie?" Sam almost shouted. "Now, wasn't it a lie?"

"Yes, sir," Will said, and put his papers in his jacket pocket.

"You right, it was."

Sam pushed back from his desk.

"That's it, boy. You can't register. You don't qualify. Liars don't qualify."

"But . . ."

"That's it." Sam spat the words out and looked at Will hard for a second and then he swung his chair around until he faced Charlie.

"Charlie."

"Yeah, Sam."

"Charlie. You want to go out to eat first today?"

Will opened the door and went out. As he walked down the stairs, he took off his jacket and his tie and opened his collar and rolled up his shirt sleeves. He stood on the courthouse steps and took a deep breath and heard a noise come from his throat when he breathed out. He looked up at the flag in the courtyard. The flag hung from its staff, still and quiet, the way he hated to see it; but, it was there, waiting, and he knew that a little push from the right breeze would lift it and send it flying and waving and whipping from its staff, proud, the way he liked to see it.

He took out a cigarette and lit it and took a slow, deep drag. He blew the smoke out. He saw the cigarette burning in his right hand, turned it between his thumb and forefinger, made a face, and let the cigarette drop to the courthouse steps.

He threw his jacket over his left shoulder and walked on down to the bus stop, swinging his arms.

Chapter

Three

Will had to wait for a bus. The bus he would take ran every fifteen minutes. He saw by the schedule posted there at the bus stop that he had to wait ten minutes. Ten minutes. That was just enough time to get a cold drink. Will's favorite cold drink was orange juice, real orange juice, not the kind with water mixed in it. Of course, if the water is in the form of ice, I don't mind that, thought Will. Come to think of it, it's pretty good with ice in it. You can suck the ice afterwards and it gives you a chance to have something cold in your mouth as you walk along in the heat.

He put the whole thing out of his mind. After all, he was in the center of town. He couldn't go in one of those drugstores and order a drink. There was a drugstore right there at the bus stop, with a fountain and girls dressed in clean white uniforms, waiting. They waited to help people get relief from the heat by serving them all kinds of cold drinks, including orange juice the way he liked it; or, if people didn't want to spend money, they could have a glass of cold water, free.

But not me. No, not me. I couldn't go in there, thought Will. I couldn't have a glass of cold water free. Couldn't even buy it. Not me. Couldn't buy cold orange juice with ice floating around in it. Couldn't even buy it even if I was very very rich.

There was a sign on the outside of the drugstore that said: COME IN OUT OF THE HEAT—AIR CONDITIONED. There were some women in there. Housewives out shopping, thought Will. The women took the sign at its word and went in. They didn't buy anything. They just stood around in there and got cool.

Cooool.

Will turned his back to the drugstore and looked down the street in the direction from which the bus would come. He did not see it. He knew he would not see it. He looked anyway.

Oh, the heat. The heat. It must be one hundred degrees in the shade and one hundred and fifty, at least, out here, thought Will. If it isn't, it sure feels like it, anyway. He hated the heat. He knew that was a crazy thing to do. He was always doing it though. Hate the heat, wish for cold. Hate the cold, wish for heat.

He remembered that time when he really did hate the

cold and prayed for the heat. It was that winter he got hit in Korea. It wasn't cold, it was freezing, the way it never did in his town. It was so warm in his town all year around he never saw a topcoat.

He hadn't been used to the cold over in Korea, but he made out all right, better than all right, against it, because the Army had taught him how to take care of himself in cold weather. He was glad he had listened to the Army when the Army taught him what to do because he knew two disabled veterans who got that way because they hadn't listened. He had listened and he had made out all right—that is, until he got hit. He always smiled when he remembered the time he got hit. It always made him think about a saying he heard someplace that went: Don't get caught with your drawers down. He always thought, too, about cowboys in Western movies who never want to die with their boots off. He knew how they felt. One of the things he had been taught to do in order to take care of his feet in cold weather was to change his socks as often as possible. He always kept a pair of socks under his jacket next to his body while he was in Korea. They were warm and dry that way. That day he got hit he had just taken off his boots and put on a fresh pair of socks and he was all set to put his boots back on when there was a surprise attack by the communists. He was hit in his chest and he didn't have his boots on. He didn't remember being unconscious. Maybe he was, maybe he wasn't. He didn't know. What he did remember was he had been sitting in a pretty dry place on a rock and after he got hit he found himself face down in snow and ice and water. The right side of his face was stuck down in that cold slush and three feet away were his boots, standing there, majestically, waiting for him to stick his now cold, wet feet down in them. His rifle was there too. He knew that, even though he couldn't see it. He didn't even remember thinking of his rifle. All he could see and think of were those boots. They stood there, side by side; tall, brown, dirty, like two dirty old buildings that had two thousand hot radiators inside. He couldn't move. He was there, face down, and he stared at those boots and he reached out for those boots and he prayed.

The fellows beat off the attack. He didn't remember any firing, but he knew there was some and that they beat off the attack because after a time they put him on a stretcher and threw his boots and his rifle on there with him and took him back to an aid station. When he got to the aid station, the medics had to work to pull those boots away in order to get to his wound. He was hugging those boots and kissing those boots and promising those boots that he would take care of them. He promised he would keep those boots clean and dry and shining and he was going to take those boots home with him where it was never cold and snowy and icy. But, when he was sent to the rear, to a hospital, they took all his clothes and his boots and he never saw them again.

Something happened to him in that hospital. Something that taught him that people can be all right, no matter who people are or where they come from, or where they're going, or what they do in life. He saw with his own eyes and he felt with his own heart the reward of the seemingly smallest kindness. There was this room they put him in at the hospital; a long room, and it had one hundred beds with one hundred wounded soldiers in them, fifty on each side of the room. Will was one of them. He was the hundredth soldier, stuck down in a corner bed. One day they got news that a movie star was there and that she was coming to their room. They were all very happy about it. They didn't know her name or what she was going to do. Some way or another they came to the conclusion that she would come in and sing and tell jokes. Will didn't care what she was going to do. She was a woman. That was all that mattered. She was a woman and being in the room was really quite enough. For all he cared she didn't have to do or say anything. Not one single thing.

Before she came somebody told the men what her name was. As soon as they heard her name they knew that she wasn't a singer or a funny lady. She was a straight dramatic actress, and a very good one too. Besides that, there was her beauty. She was very pretty.

They waited. . . .

Will wondered what she was going to do. Probably come in and yell "Hello" and smile and stand there and say "Poor things" and talk to the officer who was showing her around and smile some more and yell "Good-by. Good-by, you poor things" and walk out. What the heck? You couldn't expect any more. It was all just a publicity thing so all the folks back home could read about her in the newspapers and like her and go to see all her pictures. So what? He didn't care about that. All he cared about was she was coming. All the patients seemed to feel the same way. So much so that everyone had his head turned toward the door, even the blind fellows. They were all very quiet until she came in and yelled "Hello everybody." They yelled "Hello" back to her and smiled and grinned and waited to see just what she would do. Will hoped her visit wouldn't be too short.

There she was, all smiles and looking around, and then she took off her fur coat. I'll bet it's mink, Will thought. He didn't know anything about those things. She had on a one-piece black dress. It wasn't tight or vulgar. It was nice. It was well tailored and well fitting. Will could hear murmurings of "Oooooo" and "Ahhhhhh" and fellows who could see describing her to fellows who were blind. She gave her coat to one of the officers who came in with her and she went to a bed and took a soldier's hand and talked with him, then she went to another bed, and another, and another. By this time Will knew what she was going to do. She was going to stop at every bed in the room. She was going to shake hands and talk with one hundred fellows. She was going to talk and shake hands with him.

Me, thought Will.

Will was flat on his back. He was sweating, and waiting. He didn't quite believe she would come to his bed. He hadn't been raised that way. She came closer. Will's right hand started to sweat and feel heavy. He put it under the bed sheet and opened it and closed it. It felt very wet. He wiped it off on the sheet and it got wet again. He didn't want his hand to be wet when she took it. When she came to the bed next to his, he rubbed his hand dry on his sheet and took it out from under the sheet and hoped it wouldn't be wet when she took it.

She came, her hand out, reaching for Will's hand, and she was smiling. Will rubbed his hand quickly on the sheet once more and in that same motion he brought it up to her hand.

He didn't remember what she said. He didn't really know if he understood at the time, or if he heard clearly. It didn't matter what she said. What mattered was that she made him and all the others feel good. Real good. Only it was more than that with Will. She made him feel like a human being.

A real human being.

It was good thinking about that movie star. She was a real star, thought Will. A Star.

He felt good enough, now, to take a cigarette. He finished it just as the bus came.

He didn't want to go home. There wasn't any special thing that he wanted to do except be alone. He had to go home, though, and tell Mom how it had all ended. Besides that, he had just a half day free from work and he had to get home and change clothes and get out to the factory. They had a notice at the factory that said anyone who wanted to register to vote could have the morning free to do it.

Will had felt pretty good when he got on the bus that morning. He didn't feel the same way when he got off near home. He walked fast toward home. He thought he must have looked like he felt because some of the people in his block came to their windows and doors and watched him and then they turned away. They knew he had failed.

Mom knew it too. She met him at the front door.

"Things don't come easy in this world," she said. "Not good things. Worth-while things."

She kissed him on the right cheek.

"Remember what I said when you left this morning, son? Remember?"

Will remembered.

"I meant it," Mom said.

"I know, Mom," Will said.

"I meant it. I'm proud of you. Real proud."

Will threw his jacket on the sofa and sat beside it.

"You know what they got me on, Mom? This will kill you." He tried to laugh. It didn't come out like a laugh at all. "It'll slay you." He tried to laugh again, and failed. "Mom. Mom, I'm a full-fledged member of an organization."

"Oh, no." She sat down in a chair. "No, you're not, Will. It's one of the things we've been extra-careful about."

"Have we, Mom?"

"I've told you not to join anything. Not even the Red Cross."

"Oh, yes, Mom. We've been careful about it." Will forced a smile. "Only, only I was in this organization before we started being so careful."

"What is it? You never told me about being a member of any—"

"It's the Army Reserve, Mom."

"Oh, no."

"Yes," Will said and threw his arms up. "I don't know. I thought they would pick something better than that to get me on." He locked his hands behind his head. "I didn't even think of it. He asked me if I was a member of any organization and I said no, like a fool. Stupid. I thought he was talking about some kind of organization like the communists or some kind of organization that was trying to fight them. Anyway, who isn't in the Reserve? If he was younger or if he has a son who's been drafted into the Army, he's in it, too. I thought they might get me on something better than that."

"What did he say about it?"

"He said I lied when I said I wasn't in an organization and liars can't register to vote."

"Was it the fat one?"

"The one called Sam," Will said.

"I remember him," Mom said. "He's been there a long time."

"I'm sorry, Mom."

"Don't be sorry, son. Be proud. You know good and well many people won't even try. They don't have the guts to go down and try. You did. I told you it wouldn't be easy, son."

Will stood up and put his hands in his pockets and went to the front window. Some little boys had a ball game going out in the street. Will watched one little boy get a hit. He had known it would not be easy. But he had dreamed about it anyway. He had dreamed for two years of today. Today was to be a day of triumph. Today he was to have said, "Mom, I've registered to vote," and then he would have watched her face. He would have watched the wrinkles move under her eyes and around her mouth. He would have seen her lips part and her teeth shine that special shine the way they always did when her smile was of real happiness. And then there was Mary. He had dreamed of seeing her face too. Oh, what the heck, he thought. I knew all the time it would end like this.

"Oh, Mom," he said, "what do you stay in this place for?"

"It's our home, son. Going away won't solve any problems."

Will faced his mother.

"I know, Mom," he said. "I know. But, it would be so easy to go away from all this. You've got to admit that."

"Sure it would, son. It's the easiest thing you could do."

Will went to the sofa and picked up his jacket.

"But if everybody did that, things would never change," said Mom.

"I guess you're right, Mom."

"Never change."

"I better get to work."

Mom got to her feet.

"I'll get you some lunch while you change," she said.

"I'm not hungry, Mom."

"I'll get you some lunch," said Mom.

Chapter

Four

It was five minutes to one when Will got to the front gate at the factory. There he met Flip. Will didn't think his real name was Flip. He didn't know what it was. He had met Flip when he started to work at the factory. Flip had been there for a year when Will came. Everyone called him Flip. Old Flip was the kind of fellow who was naturally friendly with everyone. I shouldn't call him Old Flip, thought Will. He isn't old. He's my age. It's just that he's the kind of fellow that makes you want to say, "Old Flip is a regular guy." You just have to use "Old" to show that you really like him.

"Hi, Flip."

"How did it go?" Flip asked.

"It didn't," Will said. He knew what Flip was talking about.

"I knew it. I knew it."

"All right."

"I knew it," Flip said.

"Okay. Now you can say 'I told you so.'"

"I did. I did. I told you so."

Flip was five feet tall and he had a voice bigger than he was. His voice grew whenever things happened as he predicted.

They headed up the walk to the factory.

"Well, Flip, I tried."

"Yes, you tried."

"Have you ever tried, Flip?"

"Me? You kidding? What do I want to try for? I leave that for crazy people like you." Flip waved his right hand at Will. He liked to wave his hands when he talked.

"You think it's crazy, Flip?"

"I think you're crazy."

"You think so?"

"Yes. I sure do," Flip said.

"Well, if I'm crazy, then what we need is more crazy people like me."

"This is the wrong place to be crazy in. You ought to know that. Did you grow up in this state?"

"This state and this town," Will said.

"Then you ought to know. I don't come from this town myself, but I come from this state, and I know."

"What do you know?"

"I know that people are born in certain places in this world. Certain places, that's what I know, and you ought to know what your place is and don't go trying to get out of it. You can't get out of it. You ought to know that. You can't get out of it. You can't, and you shouldn't ought to try. You know what you do? You only make trouble. That's what you do. You only make yourself unhappy, and you make trouble. Trouble for yourself and everybody else."

Will didn't believe that. He couldn't see Flip's point. He couldn't understand how Flip could feel the way he did. They had had conversations on this subject before and Will had tried to convince Flip he was wrong and Flip had tried to convince Will he was wrong. Neither had been successful.

"But," Will said. "What if I wasn't born in a certain place? I mean, I don't think there's a certain place according to the Constitution . . ."

"Oh, don't hand me that high-backed junk," Flip put in. "It's just a dream. That's all it is. A dream. You ought to know that. Look at facts. That counts. Look at facts. Look at the back of your hand. Go on, look at it. What do you see? What do you see? Now, that's a fact that you can't get away from. You can't dream away from that. You can't Constitution away from that. That's real. You hear me talking? That's a fact that tells you where you belong, what you are, and how you ought to act."

"It just tells me what I am," Will said.

"Don't kid yourself. You know good and well it's more

than that. You talking to Flip, now. It tells you where you belong and how you should act, too."

"If that's true, then tell me why is it that some other people in some other parts of the United States can vote? People just like you and me."

"What's stopping you from going there if voting is so important to you?" Flip asked.

"It's not just voting," Will said. "Now that's something even you should know."

"What is it, then?"

"Justice."

"Justice?"

"Justice."

"I don't get you," Flip said.

"Flip, you don't understand. I mean . . ."

"Just some more dreamy junk," Flip put in. "You right. You right. I don't understand. I look at the back of my hand and I look at the back of your hand and I see the same thing. We're just alike. No difference at all. We're just alike, but I don't understand. All I know is that people like you make trouble, that's all. That's what you do. Make trouble. What good did it do you to go down there today? What good did it do you? You tell me that. Did it make you happy? Did you get anything out of it? Did you make something? Did it get you any money?"

"Money?"

"Money. Did it get you any money? You lost a half day's work. What good did it do you?"

"I tried," Will said. "I'm not satisfied. It didn't all turn

46

out like I wanted it to, but I tried. What the heck? I *am* satisfied. I'm happy. I'm glad I had the guts to try."

Flip laughed.

"Guts," he said, and laughed again.

When they reached the factory building, they went around to the back and went inside and downstairs to the toilet. They had their water cans down there. Each can was big enough to hold one gallon of water. They had to fill up those cans with water and take them up to the third floor with them where they worked so they could have water to drink when they got thirsty. The work was hard and it was hot and they got thirsty often. It took too much time to run down to the toilet every time they were thirsty. They weren't allowed to use the water fountain because it was for the other workers.

Will filled his can first and waited for Flip to fill his. Flip filled it and drank half of it and filled it again.

"I know the difference between us, Flip," Will said.

"What?"

"Flip, you don't mind drinking water from the toilet. I do. I want to drink from the fountain."

Flip said nothing. They went upstairs to the third floor. They put their water cans in a window on the shady side of the building. They did this so that the water would not get hotter than it was. They did it too, in hope of a cool breeze that never came. They had tried many ways to keep the water from getting hotter. Once they put the water cans beside the water fountain. The water in the fountain was ice cold and they thought that just maybe a little bit of that cold would come to their water cans. They were wrong, but the water did seem cooler. They had to move their water cans away from the fountain because once they found cigarette butts in them. They tried buying ice, but the ice melted before lunch time and because there was no place near the factory where they could buy ice again at noon, they gave that up, too. The best thing to do, they found, was to keep their water cans in the window, in their sight, so no one would throw cigarette butts in them, on the shady side of the building, and hope for that cool, cool breeze that never ever came.

They stood at the window and waited for the whistle to send them to work.

"You want to drink from the fountain?" Flip asked. "Okay. Okay. There it is," he said and pointed to the water fountain at the head of the stairs. "Nobody else is up here now. Nobody's going to see you. Go ahead."

"You still don't understand, Flip. I want to drink when I want to drink. I don't want to act like a thief."

"You're crazy," Flip said.

"So, I'm crazy," Will said. He's impossible, he thought.

"You know, there ought to be a law against being crazy like you. You know that? There ought to be a law. They need a law to protect people like me from people like you."

"You need it, Flip."

"What do I need?"

"Protection, like you said."

"Well, speaking of protection. I think you should protect your job. That's what you ought to protect."

"What do you mean?"

"Mr. Brown was looking for you this morning," Flip said. "I think he was kind of mangly mad."

"Didn't you tell him where I was?"

"Who me? I don't get mixed up in nothing. This is Flip. I just told him you said you would be here at one. I don't get mixed up in nothing."

"What's he got to be mad about? There's a big sign on the main bulletin board."

"You know how he is," Flip said. "The big boss himself can say one thing, but Mr. Brown wants to do it his own way. He probably wanted you to ask him for the time off."

"So he would say no? The sign said take off. Heck with him. He's just the boss on this floor. He don't run the whole factory," Will said.

"He runs enough," Flip said. "You know that? He runs enough. He can fire you. He can fire you any time he wants to."

Will laughed.

"Fire me for what?"

"Laugh if you want," Flip said. "It's people like you who get fired. You get fired and I'll still be here. This is Flip. That's right. I'll still be here. Be here getting my check every Friday, right on schedule. You know why? I'll tell you why. I stay in my place, that's why. I know my place and I stay in it."

"You stay in your place. You and your place."

"That's right," Flip said. "That's right." He took out

his cigarettes and offered Will one. Will took it and held a match for Flip and then Will lit his own.

"Flip," Will said. "Flip, you're always talking about your place. Your place. I mean, how is it you're so sure you know your place. Heck. How do you know that it's yours?"

"Can't you learn nothing? It's like I said before. You got to look at the back of your hand. At the facts. My Mama and Papa taught me that. Yes, they did. God bless them. They said if you want to get by in this world, you got to stay in your place."

"I still want to know how you know you have a place."

"What's the matter with you? You dumb or something? I know," Flip said. "I know I have a place. You ought to know you got a place too. I look at the back of my hand and I know what that place is. Just like you ought to know. Who goes to good schools? Who have all the money? You don't. I don't. Who makes these laws you talking about? Who wrote that Constitution you talking about? Your forefathers didn't. Mine didn't."

"If you want to look at it like that," Will said, "look at all those refugees that come here from Europe. Their forefathers didn't write the Constitution either."

"Don't mean nothing," Flip said. "That don't mean a thing, and you know good and well it don't, either. Folks who could have been their forefathers wrote it. They couldn't have been your forefathers, or mine. The back of their hand is right. Those are the kind of hands that the money and the power come into. That shows you right there where your place is. Down." He pointed to the floor. "Down, way, way down."

"I know we're down, but that's no reason to stay there."

"Oh, we'll stay there, all right."

"I don't think we will. But, as long as we have people thinking like you who we have to take with us, it'll take us longer to get up."

"Hey, don't put it on me. Don't you put that on me. Who does the firing and the hiring? Who has anything to do with all the jobs you get and don't get? Who do you pay taxes to? Who tells you that you have to go in the Army and fight? And another thing. Tell me this. The last time we got some of those European refugees in this town, who was it that got fired so those refugees could have jobs? Tell me that, now. I know you must know some of the people who got fired."

"Sure, Flip," Will said. "Sure. I know some. One of them was my uncle."

"See what I mean? See what I mean? What I been telling you all the time? Huh? What I been telling you all the time? That shows you right there where your place is. Don't it? Don't it? Just like I said, down."

"That's the kind of stuff they want us to believe, Flip. You can't really believe that."

"I can't, can I? Listen. I believe what I see. I've always believed it and I'm going to keep on believing it because it's a fact. That's right. When you see it, you know it's a fact. I remember when I was in Europe in the Army and I had some European friends, I used to tell them the facts. I didn't have to tell them, they knew better than me, but they always asked about it anyway and I told them the facts. Whenever they said they wanted to come over here and live, I always told them not to stop in New York or someplace like that. I told them to come on down home here, and live. Yes, I did. I told them to come on because it meant that they would be automatically starting out life here above me and you and half the other people down here. Now, that's a fact, and you know it, too. Don't you? You might as well admit it. You know it."

"I admit it. Sure. I agree with you, but I don't admit that we have to stay down. That we belong down. Not me, anyway."

Flip laughed.

"From what I see," he said, "you better start admitting that, too."

"Never."

"You'll just make yourself unhappy. Sad."

"Then I'll be unhappy."

"I fell when I was born and you did, too. I know it and you don't. I feel sorry for you," Flip said, and shook his head.

"You?" Will wanted to laugh. "You feel sorry for me?"

"That's right. Because you're going to have many, many disappointments."

"I'm not blind," Will said. "I know I'm going to have disappointments. I know it and I expect them. I'm the kind of person that—"

"Why?" Flip interrupted. "Why think about all this

business? Why? Just learn your place and forget about it. Stay in your place and think about other things."

"You know, Flip, if all of us felt like that you wouldn't have this job. You know that? It wouldn't have been possible for you to have this job?"

The boss, Mr. Brown, came up the stairs then, and he called Will and told him to come to his office.

Flip said, "He's still mangly mad."

"So, he's mangly mad," Will said.

Flip laughed.

Will put out his cigarette and started over to the office.

"Will," Flip called after him.

"What is it?"

"Good luck."

Will stopped and smiled at Flip and then he turned and hurried to Mr. Brown's office. There was no one in the office with him, but Mr. Brown had a rule that Flip and Will had to knock on the door before coming in.

Will knocked once and waited.

"Come in."

Will went in.

Chapter

Five

It wasn't a real office. It was just a little room with a telephone in it sitting on a little table. It had one window in the back. People who cleaned up the floors at night kept their mops and rags in the room. During the day it was Mr. Brown's castle. Mr. Brown sat behind the little table with his chair tilted back and his hands locked across his big stomach.

"Boy, you like this job here?"

Will didn't really care too much about it, but it was a job. Temporary. "I like it, all right."

"Boy, you don't like this job."

"I like it."

55

"I don't like you boys to take advantage of me. Give you the tail and you take a head."

Will didn't say anything.

Mr. Brown looked at him, hard. "I said I don't like to be took advantage of," he said, loud.

"I didn't take advantage of you."

"You calling me a lie, boy?" He let the chair fall forward with a bang and he rested his arms on the table.

"No, sir."

"You better not, boy. You just better not. If you know what's good for you."

"Mr. Brown," Will said, and waited.

"What?"

"What is this all about?"

"You questioning me, boy? Me?"

"I don't know what it's about."

"You know what it's all about."

"I don't know what it's all about."

"You know what it's about, boy. You know good."

"I'm sorry, but I don't."

"Where were you this morning?"

"I wasn't here this morning."

"I know you weren't here, boy. That's what I'm asking you. Where were you, boy?"

"I had to go down to the courthouse this morning."

"Oh, you did, did you?"

"Yes, sir."

"What kind of trouble you got in?"

"I wasn't in no trouble."

"Then what you doing down at the courthouse for?"

"I went down to register."

"What's that?" Mr. Brown asked, and leaned forward.

Will was sure Mr. Brown had heard the first time, but he said it again. "I went down to register."

"To register?"

"Yes, sir."

He was looking at Will hard now.

"Register for what?" he asked, slow.

"Register to vote," Will said, quick.

Mr. Brown stuck his chin out and looked harder at Will.

"What did you say?"

"Register to vote."

Mr. Brown laughed. He leaned back in his chair and laughed.

"You're a crazy one," he said, and laughed again. "I knew it from the first day you came here."

"No crazier than you."

"What?"

Mr. Brown stopped laughing.

"What?" he asked again.

Will said nothing.

"You trying to be smart, boy? You trying to be smart?" Mr. Brown raised his voice. "Because if you are, I can be smart too. Smarter than you." He leaned forward and lowered his voice. "Boy, you're trying to be smart with me."

"I'm not trying to be smart." Will was tired of answering that question.

"So you went down to the courthouse?"

"Yes, sir."

"To register to vote?"

"Yes, sir."

"Boy, who told you you could go down there?"

"This is the day to register."

"Who said *you* could register? Who said you could take off a half day?"

"There's a notice on the main bulletin board that says anybody who wants to register can take off the morning."

"Boy, who's your boss?"

"You."

"Boy, did I tell you you could register?"

"No, sir."

"Boy, you don't like this job here. You don't appreciate this job. Register to vote. Give you a tail and you take a head. You don't want this job."

"I want it."

"Oh, no you don't. Oh, no you don't either. You don't want it."

"I want it."

"Oh, no you don't. What you want to vote for? You took off a half day to go and register. Try and register, that is. Well, boy, I hope it made you happy, because . . ."

The telephone rang and Mr. Brown stopped talking and answered it.

"Yes, sir, Mr. Davis," he said into the telephone. "I just heard about it, sir. I've got him right here, sir. . . . Yes, sir. . . . Yes, sir. . . . Yes, sir. . . . I'll take care of it, sir. . . . Yes, sir. . . . Right away."

A smile was on his face. Will hated to look at those rusty teeth. Will saw the smile get bigger as Mr. Brown listened to Mr. Davis. Mr. Davis was the big boss.

"Yes, sir. . . . Yes, sir. . . . I'll do that, sir." He hung up. He let his right hand rest on the phone for a moment and he looked at it. Then he stood and turned his back to Will and looked out the window. His neck was thick and very red.

He laughed.

He turned around and faced Will and laughed again.

He sat down.

"Smart," he said. "Register to vote. Hah. Who do you think you are? I know the answer to that. You're one of those smart ones. You one of those who don't like things the way they are. That's what you are. You one of those who wants things to be changed. You one of those who cause trouble. I know your kind. I know your kind and I know what happens to your kind. I know. I know there're two kinds. One like Flip out there, and one kind like you. You'll learn your lesson one day, boy. You'll lean after you learn, too. Just like you ought to be. You'll learn. Smart. Smart. One day you'll learn and you'll know like Flip how to stay in your place. You'll learn what's good for you. Register to vote. Hah. That's a laugh."

"It's important to me," Will said.

"Important enough to be away from your job?"

"Yes. Yes, sir. Anyway, that sign on the main bulletin board . . ."

"That sign on the main bulletin board. That sign on the bulletin—boy, you know what that sign said?"

"I know what it said."

"Smart one. Can read, too." Mr. Brown laughed. "What did that sign say?"

"It said all men who want to register—"

"That's right," Mr. Brown said and pointed at Will. "That's right. That's what it said. 'All men.' Men. You think that meant you, boy?"

"Yes, sir."

"Boy, you think that meant you, boy?"

"Yes, sir."

"Boy. Boy, you're stupid."

"I don't have to listen to you call me names."

"Don't get smart with me, boy."

"Just what is it you want with me? I told you where I was this morning."

"I'll ask the questions, boy. Don't go asking me questions. Not me."

Will said nothing.

"You understand that?"

Will said nothing.

"Boy, that sign said 'men' and that sign meant men."

"Well, I'm old enough to vote, so I thought it meant me too."

"That's another thing. That's what's wrong with your kind. That's what's wrong. Your kind try to think. Your head and your big mouth get you in trouble."

"I'm not in trouble."

"Hah," said Mr. Brown and leaned back and laughed loud and hard.

Then he said, "That's what you think. Hah. Boy, you know what? You know what? You don't have a job."

"You mean I'm fired?"

"You heard me, boy. You heard me good and well."

Will was ready to leave. As the conversation had gone, he knew it would come to this end.

"That'll learn you, boy. Smart. Trying to be so smart to register. Trying to be so smart and you're just stupid." He laughed.

"Listen, you," Will said. "You can take this job and ram it. This isn't the only job in this town. Who do you think you are? You can't boss me outside this factory. If I want to go down to register, I'll go."

"Boy, you didn't register. I know all about it." He laughed. "I know all about it. You thought you could register? You went down and you couldn't qualify. Just like all the rest, you couldn't. Now you don't have a job to boot. That'll learn you. All of you. Besides that, boy, you won't get another job in this town. Register to vote. Hah. That's a laugh. You really think you could do that? Hah." He laughed. "Now, boy, you get out of here."

"You . . ." Will started and stopped himself. What's the use? I don't want to argue with him, Will thought. He turned and walked out. He didn't close the door behind him.

He saw Old Flip on the other side of the room, working. Flip stopped working and looked up at Will. He had a look on his face that said he was anxious to know what had happened. Will didn't want to talk to Flip. He watched Flip for a moment. Flip started to him. Will turned away from him and went to the water fountain. He looked back and saw Flip watching him. He turned to the water fountain and bent down and drank. The water was cold, ice cold, and good. As he drank, he looked to see if Mr. Brown had come out of his office. He did not see Mr. Brown. He kept drinking and he wished Mr. Brown would come out and see him. When he knew Mr. Brown would not come out, he gave it up.

Flip was still standing there on the other side of the room when Will went down the stairs. Flip stood there with his mouth open, gaping.

Chapter

Six

The day was still young and Will had time enough to
find another job. There was another factory a couple
blocks away. He went there.

"I'd like to apply for a job."

"You'd like to apply for a job?"

"Yes, sir."

"You come from this town?"

"Yes, sir."

"Where'd you work last?"

Will told the man where he had worked and the man
picked up the telephone and dialed the factory. Will
knew it would be no use. The man hung up the phone.

"Get out of here," he said.

Will left.

He went to three other places, but it was no use. They would all check with the factory and find that he had tried to register to vote and that he had been fired. It was no use. It was going to go right on being no use. Will knew that. Even so, he decided to try again the next day. He had wished that he could tell Mom he had been fired and then add that he had gone out and found another job. Now he couldn't do that. He knew it was no use. He started to hope that it really would go right on being no use. He wished they would keep saying "Get out of here" and keep throwing him out. It was the best excuse he could give Mom for leaving town. And home. He needed an excuse for Mom. I think I really wanted to escape from it all along, thought Will.

After he was thrown out of the last personnel office, Will headed for the bus stop. He had to walk two blocks to get to it. He came to a corner and waited for the traffic light to change before he crossed the street. While he stood there waiting, a woman came up. She was alone and she was blind. She had gray hair, but she wasn't really old. The gray was scattered through her brown hair and it was really the brown that Will saw first.

She and Will stood there on the corner, side by side, and waited for the light to change. Her head was turned toward Will.

"Would you be so kind to help me across the street?" she asked.

Will heard her, looked quickly at her and around her and saw no other person there, and realized she was talking to him. She stood there smiling. She had on dark glasses and her teeth were even and very white. She had a red and white cane in her right hand. Will looked up at the traffic light just as it changed. He stepped quickly into the street and crossed it. When he was a half block away, he turned and looked back and saw that the woman was still standing there, waiting for someone to help her across the street.

Will had wanted to help her across the street. He wanted very much to help her across the street. He was raised that way. It would have been a very easy thing to do. But not for me. No. Not for me. I have learned my lesson, thought Will.

He had learned long ago what kindness meant and he had learned, too, that he had to think and think good before he did something to help women, even if they needed it desperately, even if it took but a minute of his time, even if it meant their life or death.

Will had learned while he was still in the Army. It was during the time when he was almost completely well from his wound. They had sent him away from Korea and to a hospital near his home town, but far enough away to keep him from going home, except on weekends.

He had been in the hospital one month when the doctors told him that he was well enough to go out for four hours each day. The hospital was near a very small town, so small, in fact, that half the people from that town worked on the Army camp and in the Army hospital. Will knew the town couldn't be exciting because it was so small, and even if there was excitement, four hours wouldn't be enough time to really enjoy it, but he decided to go there anyway, just to see what it was like and, mainly, because it was the only place he could go to in four short hours.

There was a different system there, for Will, with the bus. He had to stand there until the other people were in the bus then he got on and paid his fare and got off again and went to the back door and got on again. Will had to have the exact fare because the driver was only allowed to give change to the other people.

Will got on and paid his fare and then he got off and ran to the back door. He had to run because there were times the driver would close the back door and drive off. If that had happened, Will would lose his money and lose his time because he would have had to stand there and wait for another bus. One of his fellow patients, who had been wounded in a leg and used crutches, had tried for an hour one day to get a bus. He was never able to make it to the back door in time. Then there was another fellow who hadn't been successful until the third bus came along. That was bad. He was an enlisted man in the United States Army and that meant he could afford to lose neither time nor money.

When Will came through the back door, there, sitting on the back seat, was a captain who had been his doctor in Korea. Will recognized him, but the captain didn't remember Will. He had had so many patients. The captain explained that he had recently been assigned to the hospital and he was going to town for the first time, as was Will.

Since it was the first time for both of them, the captain suggested they see the town together. Will agreed, and smiled to himself thinking of this. Up there it would be queer. Up there it is not done. Officers and enlisted men would not go out together up there. Overseas and up there and out there it is unheard of. But down home it is not queer at all. If these officers are down home and they want to go out, they have to be prepared to go to the same places that the naughty enlisted men go. There were only a few places they could go, officers or not. Just because they were officers and gentlemen, that meant nothing. Not down home. Just because the all-powerful United States Government said they were officers and gentlemen, that meant nothing. Not down home. When they left the Army post, that was the end of that officer and gentlemen business. Down home they were dirt. They were dirt anyway, down home, but the uniform made them even more dirt. War and in between wars, the uniform was dirt. There was no down-home hospitality for uniforms. Officers learned quickly that they had to go to a certain part of the towns—the part looked upon by the locals as dirt and when they got to that certain part they had to find the part looked upon by the locals of that certain part as dirt. Then they were home; and they had to stay in that part of the certain part and chase and play with the same women that the enlisted men chased and played. The morale of these officers must be very very low, thought Will.

When they got off the bus, they had to do it fast, Will on the captain's heels, because sometimes the driver would drive away when people were halfway through the back door. Sometimes it was wise to sit there until the bus came to a stop where many people would be using the front door. That way, there was no fear of the bus moving off when people were halfway through the back door.

"It's great to be back in the good old U.S.A.," Will said.

"The U.S.A., yes," the captain said. "This is really insane. I don't see why the Army had to build a hospital here, or anyway why they had to send me here."

"Can't you see?" Will tried to be cheerful. "The sunshine and good old down-home hospitality. And think of your patients."

"Yes," the captain said. "Well, let's not stand here. Let's take a look at the town and then I have to get back."

"Oh. You got the duty tonight, Captain?"

"No."

"Then what's your rush?"

"Do you know where we are?"

"Sure."

"I have no desire to be here at high noon, let alone at night."

"It's not that bad. Different rules from up there, but it's not that bad," said Will.

"Maybe not. I just don't like it, that's all. I felt better when I was in Korea."

Will doubted that. The captain was bitter, so Will thought that he would be quiet for a while. They walked in silence for a while.

"Not a bad-looking town," Will said presently.

"Clean."

"Say. Get a load of that."

There was a golden-haired girl one half block in front of them. From that distance, she looked very pretty.

"Reminds me of Paris, or better still, Stockholm," said the captain.

Will had never been to either Paris or Stockholm.

"Boy," he said, more at the knowledge of the captain having been in Europe than at the sight of the girl.

"Don't stare so hard," said the captain. "Remember where we are."

"Okay, but it's not that bad."

The girl stopped at the corner and waited for a car to pass and then she stepped off the curb into the street. There was another car coming around the corner and she did not see it. Will and the captain saw it. They yelled to the girl. She did not hear them. The car kept coming toward her. It refused to stop. They yelled again and again to the girl. Then she saw the car and she stopped, stood still, and screamed, her hands up to her face. The car pushed toward her. Will and the captain yelled, trying to tell her to run, get out of the way. They couldn't move either. They had stopped walking and they stood there yelling at the top of their voices. It was no use. The sight and the sound of steel against flesh against concrete told them it was no use. The car sped on.

"Come on, Doc," Will said. "Looks like you go on duty right here."

Will started to run to the girl. The captain grabbed his right arm, stopping him.

"Hold it," he said.

"Come on, Captain."

"Wait."

"Wait? But, Captain, that girl . . ."

"I know."

"Well, come on."

"Don't be stupid. Remember where we are."

"So what? You're a doctor. You going to—"

"I know," the captain put in.

". . . Let that girl lay in the gutter?"

"Yes."

"Why, Captain?"

"Those people there, now, they'll take care of her."

"But you're a doctor."

"They'll get one."

"Captain. Are you crazy? You're just standing there. You're a doctor, man."

"I know what I'm doing."

Will couldn't understand it. "You're killing that girl," he said.

"They'll take care of her."

"Doctors never say that. I'll bet you've even doctored on Red prisoners in Korea. That girl is American."

"Don't get heated up."

"What do you expect me to do? You're a captain and an officer. It's your duty to help that girl."

"Okay. Okay. I know all that, but I just can't."

"I don't care what you think of this town. This is no time to—"

"At ease. Listen to me," the captain ordered.

"Yes, sir," Will said quickly and remembered he was still Army.

"Listen. They would never let me lay a hand on that girl. They wouldn't let me near her."

"How do you know? I don't see you trying to help her."

"What are—just what are you trying to prove?" the captain asked, his face lined.

"I just expect to see you do your duty. That's all. You're standing there and that poor girl could be dying."

They stared at each other in silence for a moment, searching. Then they looked over to where the girl was. She lay still. Five men stood around. They all looked helpless. One of them took off his jacket and made a cushion for her head.

"I learned a little about first aid," Will said.

"Okay," said the captain. "Okay."

"You're going to help." Will smiled.

"Let's go over there. We'll see."

They started off, walking. Before they got there, another man ran up. "I called the ambulance," he said to the others. "Is she bad?"

"Don't know."

"Looks like it."

The girl was crying.

"Help me," she said. "Please."

"I don't think we should fool with moving her," one of the men said.

"She's bleeding," another said.

"My leg," the girl cried.

"Don't nobody know what to do for her?"

"Please," the girl said.

Six men stood around her with their mouths hanging open, lighting cigarettes, rubbing chins, scraping feet in the dirty street, kicking up dust from the concrete, putting hands in pockets, taking them out—helpless.

"Now, you just take it easy, Miss."

"The doctor's coming."

"She's bleeding bad."

"Please."

"Anybody got a car?"

"Don't think we ought to move her."

"Please. My leg. My leg."

"Now, you just take it slow, Miss."

"The ambulance is coming soon, now."

"Quiet now, Miss."

"Please. My God, please help me." She kept crying.

"Easy, Miss."

She screamed.

Will and the captain arrived. "Pardon me," Will said. He pushed past one of the men. The captain was at his heels.

"What the—" one of the men started. He grabbed Will's right arm and pushed him back against the captain.

"Where are you all going?" he asked.

"What do you think you're doing?" another asked.

"Get out of here."

"But we want to help," Will said. "He's a doctor."

"What?"

"Get out of here."

"I'm a doctor," the captain said.

"My leg, my leg. Please," the girl said.

All the men turned toward Will and the captain.

The girl screamed.

"You know what's good for you, you'll start hightailing it," one of the men said.

The others mumbled agreement.

"But I want to help. I'm a doctor."

"Don't talk back."

"I'm not going to tell you all any more," a man said.

"But he's a doctor," Will said.

"You all hear what I say?" a man yelled.

"My God. Please. Please," the girl said.

The captain moved toward the girl. The men, who were between the captain and the girl, moved forward. The captain stopped.

"You all just going to stand there? You all going to stand there?" one of the men asked, shouting.

The girl screamed.

"The girl," Will said.

"Girl? You being smart?" One of the men used both hands on Will's chest and pushed him back.

"You better git."

"Smart ones. Let's get them," another man said and moved forward.

"The girl," another said.

The man stopped. "Move," he said.

"Please. Please help me," the girl cried.

"Come on, let's go," the captain said to Will.

The girl screamed.

"Start running," a man said.

"Come on," the captain said.

They started off, walking. Will looked back at the girl.

"You want to die?" the captain asked Will. "You want to die? Let's get out of here."

Will kept looking back. "That poor girl," he said.

"Take it easy, Miss," one of the men said. He took out his handkerchief and kneeled down beside her. "Easy," he said and wiped her face.

"Help me, please. Help me."

"The doc's coming pretty soon now, Miss."

"Please. Please. God."

"Easy, Miss. Easy, now."

Will kept looking back, walking away and thinking the captain was beside him. The captain was twenty feet ahead of him, not looking back.

"I said run," a man shouted to them.

"Get a move on," another yelled.

It was then that Will turned and saw that the captain was well in front of him and beginning to run. Will ran too.

One of the men picked up a stone and he threw it at them. It did not hit them. Two other men threw stones that missed too.

"Run. I said run, you dirty . . ."

The girl screamed.

Will caught up with the captain and they ran side by side.

They ran to the bus stop and, since there was no bus in sight, they ran to the next bus stop. Will fell down just as he got in the bus because he had let the captain go in first and the bus jerked off just as Will stepped in, tripping him. They rode back to the hospital in silence. It was the last time Will had seen the captain, but he remembered him well and he had learned a lesson. Will had learned to think before helping women. That is why he had not helped the blind woman across the street. He could not know who would have seen him do it. He could not know what would happen and he did not want to find out. He could not know how many angry men would throw stones at him.

He was tired of it all.

Chapter

Seven

It was four o'clock when Will got home. He smelled cabbage cooking when he walked in the front door. Mom was in the kitchen getting supper. She was surprised to see Will home so early.

"I've been fired, Mom. They didn't like it because I tried to register to vote."

"Oh, no, Will."

"Yes, and that's not all. I don't think I'll be able to get another job in this town, either."

"You'll get another one," Mom said.

"I don't think so."

"Don't talk silly. You'll get another one."

Will looked at his mother. He couldn't say anything.

She had that look on her face. Every time he saw that look, her lips tight, her brow lined, he remembered the last time he had seen Dad. He was arguing with Mom. Will was still in short pants then, and he stood in a corner sucking his thumb, watching them face each other, that look on Mom's face as she listened to Dad yell at her at the top of his voice and then him leaving the room and Mom coming over to the corner and grabbing Will and holding him and crying, crying for a long, long time. Dad had gone, left them. Will never asked why, but over the years he had learned why.

"Mom, I'm going to take a bath."

"All right."

"I need a bath."

"Yes, you do that. I'll have supper ready soon."

"All right, Mom."

"Yes. You take your bath, son."

Will filled the bathtub with cold water and got in and stayed there. He didn't wash or move around in the tub. He just stayed there with his head and knees sticking up out of the water. He was very still and he tried not to think. He smelled the cabbage. He closed his eyes and leaned back his head and smelled the cabbage. He stayed that way for forty minutes, until Mom called him and told him that supper was ready.

"Why don't you think you'll be able to get another job, son?"

"Well, I tried this afternoon and every place I went to called up the factory and found out I tried to register. Besides, the foreman said I wouldn't get another job."

"Don't you listen to him," Mom said.

"Looks like he's right, Mom."

"He's not right, son. I know he's not right."

"It looks like it. After this afternoon."

"Don't let it worry you."

"But it does," Will said.

"Don't let it."

"Got to have a job, Mom."

"I know."

"I think I might as well face facts and get out of this town."

"No. No, don't do that. Don't even say that. Don't say that."

"Honestly, Mom. I want to."

"I told you it would be hard, son. I've always told you it would be hard. God didn't put you down here on this earth to have it easy. He didn't do it."

"I know, Mom. We were born with two strikes against us."

"That's right. That's right. God knows that's right. And you know what that means? It means that you've got to know that everything you do is going to be hard, you hear that? Hard. And you've got to expect the worst and when it's good you've got to be grateful."

"When it's good. When is it good?"

"You can't find out if you keep talking about going away."

"Sometimes I get tired of waiting, Mom."

"Look," Mom said. "I've seen this happen before." She stopped talking and frowned. Will knew what she was thinking about. "I've seen it happen before," she went on. "Many times I've seen it happen. I've seen men get told they wouldn't be able to work again in this town. I've seen some pack up and leave because of that. Without even trying. Without a try. Just going. On the other hand, I've seen some who paid that no mind and went on looking and they got another job. Don't you see, son? All these people aren't the same. They don't all have the same ideas. They don't all agree with things being as they are."

"They're very few, Mom."

"More than you think."

"Still not enough."

"Well, the thing for you to do is find them. There're some people who'll hire you no matter what other people say. There're some people who believe in the right to work and live. I know there are, son. I just know there are."

"Sure, Mom. I agree with you. There must be some. Frankly, though, I don't know if I want to take the time to find them. I don't know."

"But you must. There're too many other people who run away. That's what it is. That's all it is. Running away. Running away. You don't want to be like that. You don't want to be one of them. You don't."

"Don't I," Will said and regretted he had said it.

"No," Mom said quickly. "No, of course not."

Will looked at her for a moment.

"I guess I don't, Mom."

"Don't guess."

"All right."

"All right, what?"

"I don't," Will said.

"Of course you don't, son. You're not a coward. I think you should try. I know it. I'm sure you'll find another job, and then, when you do, I know you'll feel good about it."

"Sure."

"What I mean is, it'll be like a victory. It will be a victory. They told you you would never get another job in this town. When you go and prove they're wrong, son, when you do, you've fooled them. You've won."

"When I do," Will said with a weak laugh.

"When you do."

"If I do."

"When you do," Mom said evenly.

"Well"—Will breathed out, hard—"I hope you're right, Mom."

"I know I'm right."

"I hope so."

"I'm right."

They sat down to supper. Will was very hungry. They had cabbage greens and ham with corn bread. Will had seconds and then he had a piece of lemon pie. He liked lemon pie more than any other kind of pie, more than any other kind of dessert. He wanted another piece of lemon pie, but he held off. He wanted to wait until later, before he went to bed.

"You won't let it worry you, will you son? I mean not having a job?"

"It worries me, Mom. Yes."

"Don't let it. When you need some money, I have my pension."

"I couldn't, Mom."

"Don't talk silly. Why not?"

"It's yours."

"So?"

"I'm a man, Mom. I can't let you be supporting me. Besides, your pension isn't very much."

"It's enough."

"Don't talk about it, Mom. I can take care of myself."

"All right," Mom said, and again, "all right, son."

"Listen, Mom." Will wanted to comfort her. "I still have some money that I've saved while I was in the Army and while I was working at the factory. I have enough, Mom, for a while. I'll go on trying to find a job and if I don't get one, I'll just have to, well, I'll just have to leave here. That's all."

"Oh, I hate to hear you talk like that. I hate to hear you say that. I hate it. I hate to think of you leaving. You're all I've got."

"I know, Mom."

"I hate it."

"I know."

"I didn't raise you up to run away."

"I know, Mom."

"Not again. Not again, God."

"I know."

"Did that sound selfish?"

"No, Mom."

"Did it, son? Did it sound selfish, Will?"

"No, Mom."

"I'm not selfish."

"No, Mom."

"It didn't sound like that, did it, son?"

"No."

"It wasn't that, son. It wasn't that at all. You know that, son."

"I know, Mom."

"I'm not selfish."

"No, Mom."

"I'm not like that. I'm not selfish. You have a right to live your own life."

"It wasn't selfish, Mom."

"I didn't mean it to be."

"It wasn't."

"That's not me, son."

"I know, Mom."

"Son," Mom said. "Even when you do find another job, you can still go away if you want to. You know that. Don't you? You know that."

"Yes, Mom."

"Sure you can. I just don't want to see you run away, that's all. I didn't raise you like that. You could find a job, and, after a time, if you wanted to go, you could quit the job and go. But you won't go, will you, son. Don't leave me. You got a right to live your own life. But, son. Please. Please don't go before you've found a job. Before you've shown them they couldn't make you leave. Before your victory."

"I won't, Mom."

"Promise me, son."

"All right."

"Promise me."

"I promise, Mom."

"I knew you wouldn't leave, son. You aren't like that. I didn't raise you like that."

Will was silent.

"Are you going over to see Mary tonight?"

"Yes."

"Yes, you better see Mary."

"I am. I was supposed to see her tonight, to tell her how I registered to vote." Will laughed. "I was going to brag."

"There'll be other years."

"Sure," Will said. "Sure, there'll be other years."

"Good years," Mom said.

"I guess I'll go over there about eight o'clock," said Will.

"You do that," Mom said. "You do that, son."

Mary lived three blocks away from Will's house. Will had known her all his life. They were engaged to be married and saw each other almost every day. That was not enough for Will. He wanted to see her almost every hour. He wanted to get married right away. He didn't believe in that business of being engaged for a year or more. However, he said nothing to Mary about that. He didn't believe in letting women know that you can't live without them. He believed in acting always casual about the whole thing, even if he was very anxious.

He went to Mary's house at eight o'clock. After he had walked the first two blocks, fast, he slowed down and walked the last block casually. When he came to Mary's house, he saw her little dog playing in the front yard. The dog ran to Will and jumped up on him and Will laughed and played around with the dog for a little while, and at the same time he kept sneaking looks at the house, and one time he saw Mary looking out at him. That's where his mind was, with Mary, not with her little dog, but he wanted to act a little casual.

He went up on the porch and sat down in the swing and waited for Mary to come out. It was the start of darkness; the sun was gone. The heat would not go. When Mary came out and sat down beside him, he started the swing going, gently, and they talked.

For the first five minutes they just talked, not saying anything, really, and after that Mary asked Will how things had gone down at the courthouse. It was what Will had waited for. He told her all about it. Almost all. He told her about not qualifying to register and about losing his job. He didn't tell her that it would be hard to find another one. He told her he would start looking for another one tomorrow.

Then they started to talk about the future, as they always did, as they liked to do. Mary said that next time they would go together to register. She wasn't old enough now, but she would be when the next time came. When that time came they would go down as Mr. and Mrs.

As she talked about it, Will thought about it. He wondered whether he really did want Mary with him the next time he went down to register in this town. He wondered if there would be a next time and if he would be able to stick out until next time. He thought about Mom. "There'll be other years. Good years." Will couldn't see it. He couldn't imagine Mary being down at that courthouse. She didn't deserve that. She deserved better. She deserved the very best. The more he thought about it, the more he was convinced that Mary had to have only good things in her life and the only way for her to have the good things was for him to make them possible, not by waiting for the "good years," not by fighting for a useless cause that did nothing but waste years, young years that could be good and happy, but by going out and getting the good things for her, and the only way for them to find even the beginning of the good was for them to get married and go away.

"There'll be other years," Mary said. "And we'll do it together."

"I don't know, Mary," said Will. "I don't know."

They sat there swinging, not saying anything for a while. Will kept thinking about it all. He heard the noise from the swing as they moved forward and backward, forward and backward.

Mary laughed and broke the silence.

"What is it?" Will asked.

"Just thinking about what you said. You mean, he really asked you where you got your suit?"

She was talking about the registrar down at the courthouse.

Will laughed. "He sure did. When I told him, he wanted to know what I was doing in New York."

"That really is a good suit," Mary said.

"It better be. I paid almost a hundred dollars for it, celebrating getting out of the Army."

"Could you try it on when you bought it, Will?"

"I sure could, honey," Will said. "You know what I did? I went in a little room and I put it on and when I was through I came out and stood in front of a mirror. I was on a little stool, like, and the man came and measured me and fitted me good. After that, I took it off and they told me to come back and pick it up in a week."

"That must have been nice," said Mary.

"It sure was good," Will said. Yes, it was nice, thought Will. Mary was right. It was nice and good to go in a store and buy clothes and meet people who wanted to be sure that you had a good fit and didn't mind even letting you try the clothes on right there in the store. Sure was good, thought Will. Poor Mary. She didn't know anything at all about such goings on. Mary had never in her life been away. He had had his chance to travel around in the Army and he had seen a lot of things. Mary knew there were some places where they let you try on the clothes before you bought them, but she had never seen such a thing. In their town, they couldn't do that. They better not even think of doing that. When they went to a store to buy suits and dresses and shoes and hats, they had to be pretty sure they could tell if the clothes were a good fit by looking at them.

They couldn't bring things back to the store and exchange them or get their money back.

"And you know what you can do, Mary?"

"What?"

"You can go in the store and walk around and look and feel the material."

"With your hands?"

Will laughed. "Sure, with your hands. And you can talk with the salesman and then you can end up and not buy nothing."

"And he won't be mad?"

"No, he won't. When you walk out, he'll say, 'come again,' too."

"Really?"

"He sure will. And if you come in before some other people, they'll wait on you first, too."

"Land a mercy. You mean you don't have to wait until the other people get waited on first?"

"Nope. First come, first serve."

"That's nice," Mary said. "That sure is nice."

"When I bought that suit, you know what I did? I went in that store and I said I didn't make up my mind yet but I wanted a suit, and me and the salesman, we looked around and talked and felt the material"—Will smiled—"with our hands, for a long time."

"Did you do that with shoes too? Did you try them on too?"

"Sure did. I tried on about five pair before I had the right ones," Will said.

"That's nice," Mary said.

"It sure is Mary. It sure is nice."

"I know it must be."

"I wish we could do it here."

"Me too," said Mary. "It would even be nice if they would let us bring things back that don't fit."

"It sure would be good, Mary." For you, Mary, it sure would be good, thought Will. But it'll never be like that here, never.

Will took Mary's hands in his and leaned forward until his feet were firmly on the floor and stopped the swing.

"Mary. Mary, I didn't tell you everything that happened today. When I got fired they told me I would never get another job in this town. I went around and tried to find another job and they were right. Nobody would hire me."

"Oh, Will."

"But it's all right, honey. I don't care about it. We can go away. I can get a job somewhere else."

"What about your mother?" Mary asked.

"You know Mom."

"Yes, I know Mom."

"She wants me to keep looking until I find another job."

"You don't think you can find another one?"

"No."

"What are you going to do?"

"I told her I couldn't find one, that nobody would hire me. She doesn't believe it. She said that if I leave now, it'll be like running away. She's right, in a way, I guess. But I don't care. I still want to go. Until today, I thought I stood a pretty good chance to get registered and vote and make Mom happy. That would have made it easier on all of us. Especially Mom. She would have been happy and we could have left here. But now, I don't know. You know how she is with this voting business, all this business. But it's no use. I see now, it's no use. Maybe someday. But not now. Fact is, I don't think it'll ever be. That's just the way it is. I don't intend to waste the rest of your life, my life, here waiting.

"Listen, Mary. I feel just as strong about this as Mom. I believe things ought to be better. But I just don't want to spend my life here trying to make it better. Can you understand that, Mary?"

"Yes, Will."

"I'm just not a fighter, Mary. Not like this, anyway. I see how Mom is caught up in this and won't give it up. I don't want that to happen to me. I think it's why Dad left us."

"I didn't know that," Mary said.

"I don't know for certain, either. Mom's never told me, but I remember them arguing. I don't know what about. But I've come to the conclusion that Dad wanted us to leave and Mom didn't because she thought it would be running away. Which it is. She's right. And it makes me feel bad."

"You know I'll do whatever you want to do, Will."

"You're great, Mary. All I want is to live a good life with you. That's everything."

"Oh, Will."

"I want to have a job and work and take care of you. I want us to have a home and children. And if we want to vote, I don't want anything in the way of it. A big battle. If we want to do it, we do it. I want it to be so we can go down and do it and not worry about if we'll qualify or not. Mary, I just want us to live like people. Real people. That's all. You see what I mean?"

"Yes, Will."

"I believe somebody should do something about what's happening here. I know it's wrong and I know it won't change if nobody does anything. It's just that I'm not the one, Mary. Not like this. There must be some other way for me to help. I could have a job and give a little money to some organization to help the people who want to fight, or something."

Will laughed, thinking. "You know, I better not ever say that to Mom. She would think I was crazy."

"I don't think you're crazy, Will. I know what you mean."

"Do you, Mary?"

"Yes."

"You're great, Mary."

"Oh, Will."

"You are."

"Will. Will, I want to go. More than anything, I want to go."

"Would you, Mary? Any time I say?"

"Yes."

"I'm ready now," Will said. "I could go tonight. But I promised Mom I would find another job first. I couldn't leave her without trying."

"No, you couldn't do that."

"We'll wait a week and see how it goes. If I find a job, we'll get married in a month and leave. If I don't find one we'll get married quick as we can."

"I hope, Will, you know what I hope? I hope you don't find one."

Will laughed. "I do too, Mary. I hope every personnel office I go into kicks me out. For a whole week, I hope they kick me out."

Mary laughed too.

"But I'll be trying, Mary. I'll really try to get one, for Mom. You see that?"

"Yes," Mary said. "Yes, I see that."

"I'll be trying, but I'll be hoping, too."

"Where would we go, Will? Where would we go?"

"I don't know, honey. We'll decide on someplace."

"Someplace in the West?" Mary asked.

"Anyplace, Mary. Anyplace you want," Will said. "Anyplace where we can live like people."

"Someplace in the West," Mary said, smiling.

Chapter

Eight

Every time Will visited Mary he stayed until midnight. He stayed until midnight that night too. The time always went too fast for Will when he was with Mary. It was as if someone had taken the clock hands and whirled them around to twelve o'clock. Will always refused to believe it was twelve. He refused to believe it to himself. He never told Mary. He would tell her it was time to go as if he had just discovered the time, when all the while he had been watching the minutes fly.

Will took it easy as he walked home. It was midnight and most of the houses were dark. There weren't street lights at every corner like in most parts of the town. There was one light every two blocks. There was a light at the corner near Mary's house, but it was out. It had been out for nine months. The people in the town who repair such things had not gotten around to it. When Will crossed the street where the light had gone out, he was walking slowly. The sun was long gone and, while it was not as hot as it was during the day, it was still very hot and there was no breeze. Will was not sleepy. He was never sleepy after Mary. He was hungry. Oh, not really so hungry. He thought of that lemon pie waiting at home and walked faster. He would eat a slice of it, maybe two, more than likely two, and drink a glass of milk and go to bed and dream of Mary.

When he got to the next corner, all hell broke loose. He didn't know where they came from. There was a hedge there, and a couple of trees. Maybe that's why he didn't see them. He had passed the hedge and the trees and was about to step into the street and cross it when two men grabbed him, one at each of his arms. Will got his right arm free from one man and hit the one who had his left arm. Will hit him in the face and the man let go Will's left arm and Will saw him going backwards, off balance, when suddenly Will felt his whole head going down his throat and at the same time it was exploding at the top and the night turned red and brown and black and nothing. . . .

When Will opened his eyes, he found himself in the back seat of a car. His mouth was open. It was held open by a gag that ran through it, and was tied tight at the back of his head. Will felt the back of his head with his hands. There was a lump. It hurt. It hurt even more when he touched it. He had to use both his hands when he touched it because his wrists were tied together with a piece of heavy twine. There was a man who sat beside him. The man pulled Will's hands down away from the lump. Will was behind the driver and another man sat up front with the driver. The car was not going fast.

"Jeff," the man beside Will said, "I think he done come to."

Will looked at the man as he spoke. He was too big to have such a little voice.

"Don't you hit him, now," the driver said. "Don't want no blood on that seat, Luke. You hear me?"

"Aw, Jeff, let me hit him. Huh, Jeff? Huh? Let me hit him some more," Luke said. He was hitting Will all the time, as he spoke, little short punches in the ribs and on Will's right arm. They hurt.

"Now you take it easy back there, Luke. Don't want no blood in my car."

The car was a big, four-door model and it smelled new.

"Aw, Jeff," Luke said, and punched Will a hard one on his upper arm and quit.

"Now, take it easy, Luke," Jeff said. "I done told you. Now you take it easy. You give yourself a break. You going to have your chance."

"Yeah." Luke grinned. "Yeah," he said. "Yeah." Will heard him rubbing his hands together, fast, and laughing.

"Tom," Jeff, the driver, said, "this the first time you been out. That right?"

"Yes," the man who sat up front with him said.

"You didn't hit him yet, Tom," Luke said. "Jeff, Tom didn't hit him yet. Pay him back, Tom. Let Tom hit him. Let Tom hit him, Jeff."

"You didn't hit him yet, Tom?" Jeff asked.

"No."

"Go on, Jeff. Let Tom hit him. Let Tom hit him."

"Not now, Luke. He got time enough to hit him."

"Aw, go on, Jeff. Just one time. Let Tom hit him. Tom didn't hit him yet."

"I can wait to get him," Tom said. "Jeff don't want no blood in his car."

"So, this your first time, your first time out, Tom," Jeff said, and laughed. "I remember the old days. Wasn't a week would go by and us boys wouldn't be out. We didn't wait for them to get out their place. No, sir. We made sure they wouldn't even think of getting out their place. We made good and sure. Them was the days. Nowadays, I don't know. Don't know what's got into the young fellows around here. They don't ride like that no more."

"I do, Jeff," Luke said. "I do, but you don't hear about it because I'm by myself when I do."

"Do you, Luke?" Tom asked. "Do you by yourself?"

"Sure, I do. I catch one by himself and I'm by myself, and wham." Luke slapped his hands together. The sound rang through the car.

Will sweated.

"We used to burn them," Jeff said. "That's no bull. Burn them and hang them and shoot them full of holes. Anything we had a mind to do."

"Jeff. Jeff. I was to a burning once," Luke said. "I was."

"I'd rather just hang them," Jeff said. "Can't stand the smell of them anyway, let lone smelling them while they burn. Rather hang them, and while they dangling, take shots at them and fill them full of holes. One time we tried to count the holes. Couldn't do it. So many holes, you couldn't count them. And that's no bull."

"I like to choke them," Luke said, and in that moment his big left hand was at Will's neck. Will struggled.

"Now, Luke, you take it easy back there. You just take it easy," Jeff said. "I done told you you going to get your chance."

"Aw, Jeff," Luke said and took his hand away from Will's neck.

"I know how easy you make blood, Luke. I don't want no blood in here."

"Aw, Jeff."

"Now, you heard me, Luke. You don't be good I'll make you come sit up here and Tom can sit back there. Now, that's no bull."

Will didn't recognize the voices, the names, the men, the car, anything. He couldn't figure why they had him there and he couldn't ask them because he was gagged. It was a mistake. He was sure it was all a very big mistake. He knew it must be. He hadn't raped anybody. He hadn't tried to rape anybody. He hadn't even thought of raping anybody. It was a mistake. It had to be a mistake. He hadn't looked at any woman. He hadn't even thought of any woman, except Mary. Then he remembered. That blind woman. Oh, no. Could it be that? Could it be

97

that? He had looked at the blind woman and she had spoken to him. But even so, he hadn't answered her. He had said nothing to her. He had gotten away from her fast. Maybe that was it. Maybe that was why they had him. Maybe one of them had seen him looking at her and seen her talking to him. But he had been so careful. So careful. Ever since he came home from the Army, he had been very careful. He had heard about things like this happening and he had thought that if he was very careful it would never happen to him. But it had. It had. Either they had seen him and the blind woman or it was a mistake. They had the wrong man. They had the wrong man. They had the wrong man.

Will tried to pull away the gag and tell them they had the wrong man; tell them it was all a big mistake, but every time he tried to pull away the gag, Luke pulled his hands down and punched him in the ribs.

"Now, Luke. What I tell you? What I tell you?"

"Aw, Jeff. He been trying to get the gag off," Luke said and stopped punching Will.

"Boy," Jeff said to Will. "You leave that gag alone. Leave it alone or I'll turn Luke loose on you right now. That's no bull."

Will left that gag alone.

"He's bothering that gag again," Luke said. "Jeff. Can I hit him? Can I hit him? Huh? Can I, Jeff?"

"Go ahead."

Luke punched Will five times. Will held his hands up to his face and blocked some of the punches.

"All right, Luke," Jeff said. "Now, boy, you better leave

that gag alone. You should ought to have enough of trying to be so smart today. You been trying to be smart all day long. Going to the courthouse. Going down to register to vote. Going to looksee for jobs after you been told you won't work in this town no more. Being smart. That's what it is. Being smart. In my day, they didn't get smart. We took care of them before they got smart. We learned them to stay in their place. It costs to be smart, boy, it costs, and you going to pay the price. That's no bull."

"Jeff. Jeff."

"What you want, Luke?"

"Jeff. What's voting, Jeff?" Luke leaned forward. "Huh? What's voting?"

"You remember today when we went down to the courthouse?"

"Uh huh," Luke answered. "Yeah. I remember. I remember."

"Remember what we was doing down there?"

Luke said nothing. He thought and thought; it seemed to Will.

"I forgot, Jeff. I forgot. What was we doing, Jeff? What was we doing down to the courthouse?"

"We registered to vote," Jeff said.

"We did?" Luke asked. "Jeff, you mean at that place where I asked you to read me what it said on the door? That the place you mean?"

"Yeah," Jeff said, "and where we heard that this boy here was down there today to try to register like us folks."

"He was? He was?"

99

"That's why we got him, Luke," Tom said. "We can't let them do what us folks do."

"No we can't. No we can't." Luke almost shouted.

"We going to learn him. We going to learn them all. That's no bull."

"Let me kill him, Jeff. Let me choke him."

"Don't be greedy, Luke." Jeff laughed. "All three of us got to have a piece of him."

"I like necks," Luke said. "That's what I want. Just give me the neck."

"You going to kill him?" Tom asked. "You didn't tell me you was going to kill him."

"Don't you think we should ought to, Tom?"

"I don't know, Jeff. I don't know. This my first time going out."

"I like necks."

"What you think we should ought to do with him, Tom?"

"I don't know. I know a good one is a dead one, but I thought we was just going to just beat him up and scare him and let him take the message back to the others."

"Let me choke him, Jeff. Huh? Huh, Jeff?"

"If we kill him," Tom continued, "then nobody knows why because he can't take the message back. You see what I mean?"

"You got a point there. Course, I didn't think about doing nothing but getting rid of him for good. But you got a point there, Tom."

"I like necks, Jeff."

"Besides that," Tom said. "If we kill him he's just dead,

but if we make him suffer he'll wish he was dead to end it all. See what I mean?"

"Jeff," Luke called. "Jeff."

"What is it, Luke?"

"I like necks."

"I know it, Luke."

"Jeff. What we go down to the courthouse and register for?"

"To vote."

"What for, Jeff? Huh? Huh, Jeff? What for?"

"To vote, Luke. So's we can vote on Election Day."

"Oh," Luke said. "Oh."

"And he wants to do like us folks," Tom said.

"He can't do that. He can't do like us folks," Luke said.

Will sweated. His heart pumped.

"What do you think we should ought to do with him, Tom?"

There was silence. Will guessed that it was because Tom was thinking. Will was with Tom. It looked like he could be the one to save Will's life. Will hoped that Tom would convince Jeff that he should be beat up. Not killed. He wouldn't mind that. He wouldn't mind being beat up. He had been beat up before. He got well from beatings.

Luke broke the silence.

"Let me to him, Jeff. Huh? Let me choke him."

"Not now, Luke. I told you."

"Aw, Jeff."

"What you think, Tom?"

"Jeff," Tom said. "What do all of them like to do so much that they doing all the time?"

"I like necks."

"What you mean, Tom?"

"I mean, you know what they're always doing. What if he couldn't? See what I mean? What if he couldn't do it no more?"

"You mean . . . ?"

Jeff laughed.

"Now wouldn't that be something. That would be something. And that's no bull," Jeff said, and laughed again.

"What's that, Jeff? Jeff? Huh? Huh?"

Jeff kept laughing.

"Boy," he said, when he stopped laughing. "Boy, you just come from seeing your girl, didn't you? What you do there?" He laughed again. "What you do there? How many knotheads you planning on having? Ten? Twelve? I know you planning on many. That's the way it always is. You all always have a lot of kids. And that's no bull."

He laughed some more and Tom joined him.

"What's that, Jeff? Huh? What's that?"

"Was it good tonight, boy?" Jeff asked. "Was it real good?"

Tom kept laughing.

"Was what good, Jeff? Huh? Tom? Was what good?"

"You remember if it was good, boy? You remember, boy? You remember how it was? You remember what she said? How she breathed? You remember, boy? You better, boy, you just better, because all you going to have left is memories. And that's no bull."

Tom kept laughing.

Luke kept saying, "Huh, Jeff? Huh? Tom? Jeff? Huh? Huh?"

"Luke don't . . ." Tom laughed so hard he couldn't talk. "Luke," he tried again and kept laughing. When he could control himself, he said, "Luke don't get it."

"Huh, Tom? Huh?"

"I bet you that boy gets it, though," Jeff said. "Don't you, boy? Don't you get it? You'd rather be dead, wouldn't you, boy? You'd rather be dead and buried."

Jeff was right. Will got it. Will understood and he would rather be dead.

"Let me choke him, Jeff. Huh? I like necks."

"We not going to kill him, Luke."

"Huh? How come? Let me choke him."

"No, Luke."

"What we going to do? Beat him up? That all? Huh? Huh, Jeff?"

"Beat him up first, and then cut it off him."

"Huh?"

Will wanted to yell, "Kill me. Kill me."

"Huh? Cut what off, Jeff?"

They laughed on, loud and hard, and Luke tried to get them to explain what was so funny.

"Jeff? Tom? Huh?"

Will's heart pumped hard, but he had been thinking of escape. He had noticed that the door next to him was not locked. It was the kind of door that opened over the rear wheel of the car; its hinges were on the pole that separated the front from the back. That made it better.

"Huh? Jeff? Huh?"

Will knew the area. They were on a dark road east of town. If he could push the handle on the door down and jump out and get to his feet quick enough, he could run off into the woods. It would be hard for them to catch him in the dark.

"Huh, Jeff? Tom?"

Will's eyes were on that door handle. If he hit it just right, he knew he could make it. He had to make it. He looked at Luke.

Luke sat on the edge of the seat. Jeff and Tom were still laughing. Luke shook Tom's shoulders, trying to find out what was so funny.

"Huh, Tom?"

Now. Will hit the door handle and the door flung open and Will was going through it toward the black ground and freedom when suddenly his body stopped in mid-air and he never did hit the ground. Luke had caught his right leg and he pulled Will back upon the seat and he hit him two quick ones.

"Boy, you still trying to be smart?" Jeff asked. "You got a lot to learn. A lot to learn. That's no bull."

Luke closed the door and Tom reached around behind Jeff and locked it. Jeff kept driving.

Will settled back in the seat.

"Cut what off, Tom? Huh? What was Jeff and you talking about?"

This set Jeff and Tom to laughing again.

"Aw, Jeff. Huh? Cut what off?"

"Luke," Jeff said. "What is it they like to use all the time that we can cut off?"

"What they like to use?"

"Yeah."

"What they like to use. What they like to use."

"Yeah."

"What they like to use that we can cut off?"

"That's what I said."

Luke was silent. He twisted his neck and looked at Will and thought and thought.

"Jeff, you mean . . . ?"

Jeff and Tom laughed.

"You mean, you mean we going to cut off his . . . that we going to cut off his . . . ?"

"That's right," Tom put in. "Now you catching on, Luke."

Luke laughed.

"I catch on easy," he said. "I do."

All three of them laughed.

"He won't be able to operate no more. And that's no bull."

"That's what we should do with them all," Tom said. "When they're born, we should do it. Then they couldn't make no little ones to grow up and try to be smart."

"You mean he going to be going around without a thing?" Luke asked.

"That's right," Jeff said.

"He won't have a thing," Luke said.

"Not a thing," Jeff said.

"Not a big thing," Tom said.

"Not even a little thing," Jeff said.

"No thing. Nothing," Tom said.

"And that's no bull."

"Going round without a thing."

"Boy," Jeff said. "How you think you going to like it? How you think you going to feel when you don't have a thing? Think you going to feel like going on down to the courthouse? Think you going to feel like registering? Think you going to feel like being so smart? Think you going to feel like doing it?"

They all laughed.

"Think your gal going to like it? Think she going to marry you, and you without a thing? You think so, boy? Anyway, now you can find out if it's true love. Now you can find out if she really loves you. You can go to her and tell her you don't have a thing and then see what she says. I bet she won't want you then. None of them going to want you then, boy. None of them. And that's no bull."

They all laughed.

By this time Will had really made up his mind. There was only one thing for him to do. He had never thought the time would come for him to do it, but now the time was here. He had made up his mind long ago, when he was fighting in Korea. He had seen a bullet do that to a buddy. His buddy had lived, but Will had made up his mind that day and it was made up now. When they went through with their plans there was only one thing for him to do.

Suicide.

Jeff stopped the car and they all got out. Jeff had a flashlight and he led the way into the woods. Luke had Will's
left arm and he and Will followed Jeff. Tom brought up
the rear.

"Jeff. Jeff."

"What is it, Luke?"

"Jeff. Tom didn't hit him yet. Can Tom hit him now?
Huh, Jeff? Let Tom hit him."

"I don't care, but don't you let him get away, Luke.
You be careful."

"I got him, Jeff. I got him. He can't go nowheres."

Luke stopped and got behind Will and held Will's arms
and pulled him around until he faced Tom.

"Go on, Tom, hit him. Hit him like he done you. Jeff said it was all right. Go on. You didn't hit him yet. Go on, Tom."

"All right," Tom said. "You holding him, Luke? You holding him good?"

"I got him, Tom," Luke said, excited, holding tight Will's arms. "I got him. Go on."

"You got him good?"

"I got him, Tom. Go on. Hit him."

"Hold him, now."

"Hit him good, Tom."

With that, Tom hit Will in the face. It was dark and Will could not see the punch come. After being hit by Luke, Tom's punch was nothing.

"Hit him again, Tom. Go on."

"Hold him good, Luke."

"I got him."

Tom hit Will again in the face. Luke held Will so tight from behind that his body was flat up against Luke's front; the back of Will's head rested on Luke's chest. Luke laughed softly. Will could feel Luke's big stomach move as he laughed.

"Come on," Jeff called. "What you all doing back there? Come on here."

Jeff had gone on into the woods. Luke pulled Will along fast toward Jeff's flashlight. Tom came behind.

"This looks like a good enough spot," Jeff said, after they had caught up with him.

"Hold this, Tom." Jeff gave his flashlight to Tom.

"Hold him, Luke," Jeff said.

"I got him, Jeff. I got him good. Go on."

Jeff hit Will two quick ones in the face. He must have had on a ring because Will felt an extra sting. Jeff's punches were harder than Tom's and Will really felt them. Still, Luke's were harder.

"Boy, we going to learn you about being so smart. And that's no bull."

Jeff kept punching. Will had been hit in the face before in his life and had never bled. He bled now. He didn't know whether the blood came because his mouth was held open by the gag, making his skin tight, or if it was because Jeff had a ring on one of his fingers.

"Let me hit him now, Jeff." Luke whirled Will around until he faced him and then he turned him loose and in that same instant Luke hit him in the face and the next thing Will knew he found himself on the ground being kicked a hundred times.

"Hold it," Jeff said. "We don't want to kill him."

"Aw, Jeff. Let me choke him. Huh, Jeff? Huh? I like necks."

Will felt one last good, hard kick and then they all stopped.

"You know what we said we going to do to him, Luke."

"Huh? What we going to do, Jeff? Huh?"

"You remember, Luke."

"Yeah, yeah. I remember," Luke said, and then, "I think."

Will listened. As they had kicked him, he had turned over until he was face down. His hands were still tied together. They were under his body.

"Well," Tom said. "Let's get it over."

"Yeah," Jeff said. "Let's get it over."

"I think I remember, Jeff. I think."

"You got a knife?" Tom asked.

"Not on me." Jeff said. "You got one, Luke?"

Luke said nothing.

"Luke. You got one?"

"Huh? Huh? What's that? Got what?"

"A knife."

"I got a knife," Luke said. "I got a good hunting knife, I have. Never been used before."

"Let's see it," Jeff said.

"My knife?"

"What you think?"

"It's at home. I keep it right with my gun so I don't forget it when I go hunt. That's where I keep it."

"You don't have a knife with you? What you say you had a knife for?" Jeff asked. He almost shouted.

"I have too got a knife," Luke said. "I have. Brand new knife, too. At home, right with my gun. I have."

"Aw, Luke," Jeff said.

"Huh, Jeff? Huh? What's the matter, Jeff?"

"I got one in the car," Jeff said. "I'll get it out."

"What's the matter, Jeff. Huh? You mad?"

"I'll be right back," Jeff said and left.

"What's the matter with Jeff, Tom? Huh? Huh, Tom? What's the matter with Jeff?"

"You know Jeff, Luke."

"Yeah. Yeah. I know Jeff. I do. I knowed him for a

long time. What's the matter? Huh, Tom? What he mad for?"

"He's not mad at you, Luke."

"I'm glad," Luke said. "I'm glad. I don't like Jeff to be mad at me."

"He's not mad at you."

"You think he mad at me, Tom? Huh? You think so?"

"He's not mad at you, Luke."

"You don't think he mad at me?"

"No, Luke."

"I don't like Jeff to be mad at me."

"He's not mad at you."

"I'm glad. I'm glad, Tom. I don't like Jeff to be mad at me for nothing."

They were silent. Tom kept the flashlight on Will. Will wasn't silent. He moaned from his wounds.

"I like necks, Tom. I like necks."

"Yeah?"

"I wish Jeff would let me choke him. I do. I like necks."

"He's going to get worse than that," Tom said.

"I want to choke him. I want that neck."

"Take it easy, Luke."

"I like necks."

"Well, kick him instead, until Jeff gets back."

That was all Luke needed. He laughed and started to kick Will again and again.

"You too, Tom. You too. Come on."

"Luke. What you kicking him for?" It was Jeff, back. "I told you we wasn't going to kill him."

Luke stopped kicking.

"Aw, Jeff."

"I want him to feel it when we cut it off him. I don't want him knocked out."

When Will heard that, he stopped moaning.

"You get a knife?" Tom asked.

"Yeah."

"I like necks."

"Now, Luke, you be good. I done told you. You remember what we said we was going to do with him."

Luke was silent.

"Don't you remember, Luke?"

Luke said nothing.

"You remember, Luke."

"I forgot, Jeff. I done clean forgot. What we say we was going to do with him?"

"Aw, Luke."

"Huh, Jeff? Huh?"

"I done told you, Luke. We going to cut it off him."

"Now I remember, Jeff. Now I remember."

"All right, Luke."

"I remember good."

"Here's the knife, Tom."

"I don't want it," Tom said.

"Your idea, Tom. I figured you should ought to be the one to do it."

"I don't want to do it, Jeff."

"It's your first time out, Tom."

"That's all right. You can do it, Jeff."

"It's your idea, Tom."

"It's my idea, but you can go ahead and do it."

"Well, now, Tom . . ."

"He quit groaning," Tom put in.

"What?"

"He quit moaning."

"Maybe he passed out," Jeff said. "See, Luke? See? See what you done? I told you. Didn't I tell you, Luke? Didn't I?"

"Aw, Jeff."

Will braced himself. He didn't want to make a sound when they tried to find out whether he was conscious. Maybe he could figure up something or other while they waited for him to come to again.

"Kick him."

Two kicks came, the first one soft, the last one hard. Will didn't make a sound.

"He's out," Jeff said. "See, Luke? See what you done? See what you done, Luke?"

"Aw, Jeff."

"Don't 'Aw, Jeff' me."

"Maybe he's playing possum," Tom said.

"Oh, one of them smart ones," Jeff said. "We'll soon see."

Jeff kneeled down to Will's head.

"Hold the light down here," he said.

Will braced himself.

"We'll find out."

Will felt a sharp pain in the back of his neck.

He moaned.

"Trying to be smart," Jeff said and got up. He kicked Will once on the shoulder.

Will felt the blood running out of his neck. He thought he heard it dripping on the ground. That knife was sharp.

"He come to, Jeff," Luke said. Excited. Happy. "Hear him, Jeff? Hear him, Tom? He done come to again."

"I know it Luke. He don't get smart with me. And that's no bull."

"He done come to."

"That knife real sharp, Jeff?" Tom asked.

"It's sharp enough, I guess, but I was still thinking back at the car that it would be better if we had a razor. We should ought to use a razor."

"Yeah," Tom said.

"I got a razor," Luke said. "I got a brand new razor. I have. I bought it two weeks ago. A brand new one. I have."

"Yeah?"

"But I can't use it. I can't use it at all."

"How come, Luke?"

"It's a lectric razor. A real lectric razor and I bought it, but I forgot we don't have no lectric at our house."

There was silence for a moment.

"I have. I have. It's real pretty, too. Want me to tell you how it looks? Well, it's pink. That's what it is. Pink. It's a real pretty pink one."

"Here you go, Tom," Jeff said. "Go on. Cut it off him."

"I don't want to. I told you, Jeff."

"You thought it up, Tom. It was you."

"That's all right. You can do it."

"Your first time out, Tom. You should ought to do it."

"I don't want to do it, Jeff."

"Now, Tom, we don't want no bull about it. A man's first time out, it wouldn't be decent if you didn't let him do it. That's the way it is. That's just the way it is. Always been that way. Just wouldn't be decent. Not a bit."

"I don't mind, Jeff."

"Just not decent, that's all, Tom."

"I don't want to do it, Jeff. Let Luke."

"Me and Luke, we could just as soon do it, Tom. But we got our manners. First time you been out. Just not decent for us to go and do it in front of you like that. A man just don't act like that if he's a gentleman. You should ought to know that, Tom."

"I know it, Jeff. And I appreciate it. I won't take no offense if one of you all do it in my place."

"I got my manners, Tom. I just won't do it in front of you like that. I wasn't born that way. I just won't do it in front of you like that, Tom. And that's no bull."

"Well, let Luke do it then."

"Yeah, Luke," Jeff said. "You do it, Luke."

"Can I do it, Jeff? Huh? Can I? I want to do it, Jeff."

"Sure you can, Luke."

"I like necks."

"Go on, Luke."

"Now, Jeff? Can I do it right now?"

"Sure you can, Luke. Me and Tom, we'll hold him while you do it. Here's the knife."

"What for?" Luke asked.

"What for? So you can do it. What you think?"

"I do it with my hands," Luke said. "I take his neck and I—"

"You not going to choke him," Jeff said.

"What I'm going to do, Jeff? Huh?"

"Like we said. You remember, Luke."

"I forgot, Jeff. What was it we said?"

"Cut it off him. Cut it off him."

"Me?"

"Yes."

"Cut it off him right now?"

"Yes."

Luke was silent.

"Here you go, Luke. Come on."

"Aw, Jeff."

"What's the matter?"

"I like necks."

"Come on, Luke."

"Aw, Jeff."

"You said you wanted to do it, Luke."

"I like necks."

"Next time, Luke. Now take the knife and cut it off him. Here. Now take it and go on."

"Aw, Jeff."

"Go on, Luke."

"Aw, Jeff. I don't like to touch a thing."

"Don't you touch yours?"

"That's different."

"It's no difference. A thing is a thing."

"Come on, Luke," Tom said. "Take the knife."

"Aw, Tom."

"Luke, listen here, to me."

"Yeah, Jeff. Huh?"

"Don't you like to come out with me, Luke?"

"I always like to come out with you, Jeff."

"Don't you want to come again, Luke?"

"Yeah, Jeff. Yeah. I like to, with you, Jeff. I like to come with you."

"All right," Jeff said. "All right."

"I like to come out with you, Jeff."

"Well, take the knife then, Luke."

"Aw, Jeff."

"Go on, Luke."

"I like necks, Jeff."

"I know, Luke. I know you like necks. Next time you can have a neck. Next time you can have two necks."

"Can I, Jeff?"

"Sure you can."

"Can I, Jeff? Huh? Can I?"

"Sure, Jeff said it didn't he? So that's no bull."

"Can I have two necks, Jeff? Can I? All to just myself?"

"Sure you can, Luke."

"When, Jeff? Huh? When?"

"Next time we come out."

"You promise, Jeff? Huh? You promise I can have two necks?"

"It's a promise, Luke."

"When that be?"

"Next time, Luke."

"When?"

"I don't know."

"Tomorrow?"

"Not tomorrow."

"When, Jeff? Huh?"

"I don't know. Maybe next week."

"Next week? Can I have a neck then? Can I have two necks just like you said?"

"Sure, Luke. That's what I said. And you know I don't bull. Now go on and take the knife."

"Aw, Jeff."

"You want a neck, don't you? Two necks?"

"Yeah. Yeah. I like necks." Luke almost shouted.

"Okay, then. Go on and cut it off him."

"Aw, Jeff."

"Luke," Jeff said quietly. "Luke."

"Aw, Jeff."

"Now go on and cut it off him."

"All right, Jeff."

Will felt his body being pushed. They turned him over until he was on his back.

"Go on, Luke."

Luke said, "Jeff. Two necks?"

"Yeah. Now go on, Luke."

Will rolled back over onto his stomach. He was turned on his back again and Jeff pinned his shoulders to the ground. Tom had Will's ankles.

"Go on, Luke."

Luke had to pull Will's hands away. Every time he pulled them away, Will put them back. Once when Will put them back, Luke cut them. Will put them back again and again. He would rather cut hands.

"His hands in the way, Jeff."

"Well, move them."

"I done it, but he keeps on putting them back, again."

"Aw, Luke."

"Anyway, too, I can't see," Luke said.

"What you need to see for?" Jeff asked. "Just grab it and cut it off him. We can't hold him and the light too."

"Can't I do it without touching it, Jeff?"

"Wait a minute and I'll hold his hands."

Jeff let go Will's shoulders and took Will's hands and brought them back behind his head and held them down.

"All right, Luke."

"I can't see, Jeff."

"Aw, Luke," Jeff said. He let Will loose and stood up. Tom and Luke stood up too.

Will took this chance to turn over on his stomach. He saw the flashlight on the ground, shining, two feet away. Someone picked it up.

"Listen," Tom said. "I'll put the light up on top of this bush and it'll be shining right down on top of him."

"That's a good idea," Jeff said. "Maybe Luke can see now."

They rolled Will back over and pinned him down.

"Now you can see. Go on, Luke."

"Look at the blood," Luke said. "Whooo, look at the blood."

"I see it," Jeff said. "Go on."

"Look at the blood, Tom," Luke said.

"Go on, Luke," Tom said.

"Don't you want to see, Tom? What you got your back turned that-a-way for? Huh?"

The first time they had pinned Will down, Tom had Will's ankles and he faced Jeff at Will's head. Now, Tom had his back turned to Jeff. Tom faced out to the woods.

"Go on, Luke," Tom said.

"You don't want to see?" Luke asked.

"Tom, turn around," Jeff said.

"Look at the blood," Luke said. "Whoooo, the blood."

"I don't want to," Tom said. "Go on, Luke, get it over."

Will didn't know what Luke was doing. He couldn't feel Luke touch him.

"Look at the blood, the bloooood," Luke said.

"Go on, Luke."

"Don't you want to see, Tom?" Luke asked.

"No."

"I don't want to do it if you don't look."

"I don't want to look."

"Tom," Jeff said. "Tom, turn around."

"No."

"It's no fair, Tom, if you don't looksee. I can't do it if you don't looksee."

"No."

"Come on, Tom," Jeff said. "Turn around so he can do it."

"No."

"Go on, Luke, cut it off him," Jeff said. "Tom, he don't need to see."

"Whoooo, look at the blood."

"Maybe he's bleeding to death," Tom said to the woods.

"When I cut it off him there'll be some more blood,"

Luke said. "Won't it, Jeff? Won't it be some more blood when I cut it off him? Won't—"

"I don't care. Go on, Luke," Jeff said.

"Tom, turn around now and see me do it. Come on, Tom. Huh? Huh, Tom?"

"No, Luke. Now go on and get it over."

"Aw, Tom. Come on. Huh?"

"I don't want to see it. I don't want to. Now go on, Luke, get it over."

"Won't be no fun if everybody don't see. Won't be no fun at all. Will it, Jeff? Will it be no fun?"

"Go on, Luke," Jeff said. "Cut it off him."

Will felt Luke's hand touch him and he tried to twist away. It was no use. It was no use at all. They had him pinned to the ground. They had him pinned good. Will wished he would faint. Will wished and wished. It was no use. He could not faint.

"Go on, Luke."

"Aw, Jeff."

Will didn't feel Luke's hand there any more.

"Jeff," Luke said. "Jeff. Jeff. I like necks and I appreciate it because you let me go out with you all the time, but I can't touch a thing, Jeff. I just can't, Jeff. That's all. Don't be mad at me, Jeff, because I can't touch a thing, Jeff. I just can't touch a thing."

"Oh, the hell with it," Jeff shouted. He got up and walked away.

"Jeff. Jeff. Jeff, don't be mad at me. Jeff. Jeff. Jeff," Luke said.

Tom let Will's ankles loose and stood up. Will turned over on his stomach.

"Don't be mad at me, Jeff. Huh, Jeff. Don't be mad at me, Jeff. Jeff. Jeff," Luke said.

"Bring my flashlight." Jeff's voice came from a distance.

"I'll get it, Luke," Tom said.

"Tom, Jeff's mad. Real mad. Jeff. Jeff," Luke called. "Jeff. Jeff, don't be mad at me."

"Come on, Luke," Tom said.

"Jeff's mad, Tom. Real mad."

"Let's go, Luke."

"Jeff. Jeff. Jeff, don't be mad."

Will heard them walk off. He tried to get to his feet. He got to his knees. He could not get to his feet.

"Jeff. Don't be mad. Jeff. Jeff. I just like necks. Huh, Jeff? Huh? Don't be mad at me, Jeff."

Will crawled. He did not want to be there when they came back. He came to a small tree. He pulled himself up until he was on his feet. After he got to his feet, he found that he could not move. His body ached all over and he was very tired.

"Don't be mad at me, Jeff. Huh? Don't . . ."

Will heard the car start and doors slam and wheels screech and the motor race.

They were gone.

Will used both his hands to take away the gag. He could not take away the twine that bound his wrists. After he had taken away the gag, he made his way by grabbing tree after tree. He stopped at one tree and held it and looked up through the treetops. He could have sworn he saw the sun. He went to the next tree, and the next, and the next.

Chapter

Ten

Will struggled on for fifteen minutes. He was tired and he ached all over, especially his head and hands. As he went he held his hands out in front of him, reaching for another tree. When his hands touched a tree the pain from the touch shot up his arms and exploded just below his elbows. He had to take his hands away from the trees fast and lean on the trees with his shoulder. As fast as possible he took deep breaths and put his hands out in front of him again and moved on to the next tree.

During those fifteen minutes there was only one thing in his mind. Go. Go. Go. Get as far away from the spot they had him as possible. Go. Go. Go. It didn't matter what direction he went. Just as long as he stayed in the woods and kept moving away from where they had had him. Go. Go. Go.

When Will thought he was far enough away that they couldn't find him if they came back, he stopped and held his breath and listened. All he heard was quiet. He sat down and leaned his back against a tree. He held his breath and listened again. Quiet rang in the woods. He put his head back against the tree and breathed hard through his open mouth. He let his legs stretch out in front of him, flat on the ground, and breathed. All he could hear was himself breathing quick and hard.

After a while he started trying to get the twine off his wrists. He started biting the twine. As he bit into the twine, his hands rubbed against his face. The pain was running wild in his hands and they were wet. He stopped biting the twine. He smelled his hands. He kept smelling his hands, hearing himself sniff, sniff. He couldn't figure what it was. He couldn't decide whether there was a smell or not. He rubbed the back of his hands on his face. The pain got wilder. He remembered that he had been cut by Luke. He put his hands to his mouth and licked them and knew it was blood. He let his tongue slowly move over the backs of his hands and he counted the cuts. There were three on the back of his right hand and two below his left thumb. His tongue kept going and found that there was a gash on his right wrist, between the twine and his hand.

He thanked God that he had been in the Army. Suppose he had never been in the Army? Suppose he had never been in war? Suppose he had never been where he could see wounded men? Suppose this had happened to him before he went into the war? Suppose I hadn't learned a little about first aid, Will asked himself. Thanks for the Army and thanks for the war, thought Will.

He had caught his breath. He could think now. The best thing he could do now was to leave his wrists tied. The twine served as a tourniquet. Thanks for the war. And rest, too. He didn't feel tired, but he couldn't tell. He felt scared. Maybe that was the same thing as being tired. Scared of what has happened. Tired of what has happened. He took a deep breath. He breathed out, hard. It was like blowing out his thoughts. Can't be thinking crazy now, he thought.

He remembered a handkerchief he had in his back pocket. He could get it and tie it around his wrist. Which pocket? It must be the right pocket, he thought. He tried to get to it. He couldn't do it. I could let my pants down and get to it that way, he thought. He started to get up and do that. Oh, what the heck? He leaned back against the tree. He brought his hands up to his chest and his right hand grabbed his shirt and he bent his head down and took the shirt from his hand with his teeth and tore it. He took the torn bit with his hands and pulled until he had ripped off a piece of his shirt. It would serve as a tourniquet in addition to the twine. He tied it on his right arm with his teeth. His left hand was not cut as bad as his right and his left wrist was not cut at all. Since he had two long ends left over after he had tied his right arm, he decided to make a tourniquet for his left arm, too. I don't think my left arm needs it, he thought, but I'll do it anyway. It sure can't hurt.

After he had finished with the tourniquet he sat quietly and made plans. It was still dark, but it was getting lighter all the time. The first thing he had to do was make his way back to the road. Not on the road. He would not go on the road. He would stay off the road, just far enough in the woods so that he could see the road. After that, getting home would be nothing.

Getting home. And then what? Then leave, leave as fast as he could. But first he had to show Mom. Let her see him just as he is now. Let her see every detail. See what you done, Mom? See what you done, Mom? See what you done to me, Mom? You. You, Mom. Yes, you. Because you wouldn't let me go when I wanted to. You made me stay. You did it. You did it. Mom, you did this to your son.

Was that the right thing to say? Could he say that to Mom? Was it true? Yes, it's true.

No. No, it's not.

Oh, I don't know. I don't know.

I don't know.

Will got to his feet and started walking. It wasn't easy. It wasn't as easy as he had thought it would be. Maybe he hadn't rested long enough. Sure, that's it, he thought and sat down again. Just a few more minutes rest.

Thanks for the war.

Thanks for Mary, too. Nice Mary. Nice Mary. Sure is nice. That's all I want, Mary. You. You. That's all I want.

You understand that, Mary? Nice Mary. That's all I want. You're all I want. I don't want to fight nobody. I don't want to fight nobody.

"I don't want to fight nobody."

I don't want to fight nobody at all. What I want to fight for? You know that, Mary? I don't want to fight nobody.

Unless it's you, Mary. Unless it's you I'm fighting. Unless I'm fighting you in bed.

Will laughed out loud.

He stopped laughing and struggled to his feet.

I'm sorry, Mary.

"I'm sorry."

It was still hard for him to walk. He wished his hands were all right so he could tear a limb from a tree and use it to walk with. He stood still for a moment, trying to steady himself. He didn't want to sit down again. He tried to steady his legs. It was like that time he got drunk. That time when he first went into the Army. That time when he wanted to do what all the others did.

He couldn't stand there. He had to get moving. Go. Go. Go again. He started out. He found he had to do as he had done before; go from tree to tree. As he struggled from tree to tree he held his arms up, thinking the blood would not run out that way.

He kept going.

See what you done, Mom? See what you done to me? You did it, Mom, he thought, and it was as if he faced her and shouted the words out to her.

You did it, Mom.

Did you do it, Mom?

Yes, you did.

Did you, Mom?

I don't know. I don't know, Mom. Oh, Mom. You couldn't do this to me, your own son. You couldn't.

You didn't do it, did you, Mom?

Oh, I did it by coming back here. I did it myself. I shouldn't have come back. I should have stayed away.

He kept going until he found the road. He knew he was near the road when he heard a car. Getting home would be nothing now. All he had to do was follow the road.

I'm coming, Mom. I'm coming home, Mom. I'm coming.

He went down. He got up and went from tree to tree in the woods twenty feet from the road. He had tried to keep his arms up. They would not stay up now. He could not hold them up. It was lighter, now, and he could see. He looked down at the tourniquet. It was red. Soaked with blood. He stopped when he saw it and leaned against a tree and stared at it.

Can't stand here. Got to keep going. I'm coming, Mom.

He heard a car.

He fell to the ground and stayed there until the car was gone. He tried to get to his feet. Then he discovered that he could feel nothing with his hands. He couldn't even feel the wounds any more. His hands were numb. He stayed there on the ground, motionless, for a moment.

He rolled to the nearest tree and used his shoulders

and legs and the tree to get to his feet. Then he started out again.

Then there was another car and he had to fall to the ground once more to keep from being seen. He stayed there for a long time after the car had gone, thinking.

They wouldn't be out there now, looking for him. It's morning. It's almost six o'clock. Wouldn't they be gone now? Wouldn't they? Why stay in the woods?

He thought of Mom's words, "All these people aren't the same."

Maybe he should go out to the street and maybe a car would come along and then they would stop and pick him up and take him to a hospital.

I don't want to go to the hospital. I want to go home. I want to go home. Mom. Mom. I want to go home.

I'm coming, Mom. I'm coming home again.

Will tried to get to his feet. He rolled his body over to a tree to try as he had done before. This time his legs would not stay together as he rolled and after each roll he had to drag his legs together again before he could continue rolling. When he had come to the tree, he raised himself up on his right elbow and put his shoulder against the tree and tried to push himself up. He fell on his hands and the pain bombed his arms below his elbows. He yelled out and turned over until he was on his back and gritted his teeth until the pain was small again. Then he tried to get to his feet once more. He was careful not to fall this time, but he could not get to his feet. It was like trying to pull up a tree from its roots with bare hands. He gave it up and let his body fall until he was on his back staring up through the treetops.

He stayed that way and cried. He cried for a long time.

He cried until he heard another car coming. He worked his legs, hands, feet, back, mouth until he knew he could get nowhere. He shouted, "Help. Help, Help," until he couldn't hear the car any more.

He stayed quiet for a moment, thinking. He had to get to the road. He had to. Nobody would see him here. There was only one way for him to get to the road. Roll. He had to roll out there.

He started out.

I'm coming home, Mom. I'm coming home. Here I come, Mom. I smell cabbage greens and ham cooking. You know I'm coming now, Mom. Here I come, Mom. Coming home.

It took Will half an hour to get out to the road into the ditch. He had to roll and rest and draw his legs together and roll and rest and draw his legs together.

He was on his back in the ditch now, and he could see the sky turning blue. The side of the ditch looked like Mount Fuji he had seen in Japan. He tried once to get up the side of the ditch and failed. He tried again and this time it seemed as if the side of the ditch had grown. He gave it up.

Then he heard another car coming. He tried again to get up the side of the ditch. It was no use. The side of the ditch was even higher now. The car got nearer and Will shouted for help. It was work, but it did not matter. He kept it up.

The car sped on.

Will lay quiet, waiting for the next car, watching the side of the ditch grow.

Then he heard steps, heavy steps, slow steps. He tried to raise his body and when that failed he tried to raise his head. His head came up, but he couldn't keep it up long and he didn't want to. What he had seen was enough. Will smiled. He was happy now.

When he raised his head, he had seen a horse and behind the horse a man sitting on a wagon and the man's face had made everything all right again.

In a moment, the man was standing over him, looking down at him. It was an old man.

"Lord have mercy," the old man said. "Them folks been at it again. Why don't they leave us folks alone?"

He kneeled down and looked closer at Will. Will tried to smile to show that he was happy.

"Still living," the old man said. "You must be a lucky one, still living. You know that? You must be a lucky one."

"Take me home," Will said. "Take me home, please."

"Looks like lynching to me. Them folks sure been at it again. Now, you just take it easy, young fellow. I'll put you on my wagon and take you to a doctor. Lord have mercy. Lord have mercy. You lucky to be living. You know that? Plumb lucky. Can you talk? I said, can you talk?"

"Sure I can talk. I can't stand up, but I can talk," said Will.

"No, I guess you can't talk. All that blood. No wonder

you can't talk. I wonder what they did to you. Wonder what they got you for."

"I can talk. I can talk. Don't you hear me? What's the matter with you?"

"I don't know how I'm going to get you on the wagon. Sickness, you know. Been down in the back. I don't know. Old age, I guess. But don't worry, I'll get you up there, though."

"Maybe if you help me to my feet, maybe I can stand up," Will said.

"Now, let's see," the old man said. "Maybe if I help you to your feet you can stand up. What do you think of that?"

"Yes, yes. That's what I said," Will said.

The old man went to Will's head and put his hands under Will's arms and raised him until he was sitting up.

"I'll draw up my legs and push up," Will said. "You hold steady, now."

"Now see if you can push up with your legs," the old man said. "I'll try to raise you up when you do."

Will tried to draw his legs up. He tried and tried. His legs would not move.

"I can't do it," he said. "I can't move my legs."

"Either you weak or you can't hear what I'm saying," the old man said. "Looks like I'll have to drag you up there."

"What's the matter with you, old man?" Will asked. "Can't you hear?"

The old man pulled Will up on the road. Will's heels dragged in the dirt, making two lines in the dirt. When they were up on the road beside the wagon, the old man sat Will down so that Will's back and head rested against a rear wheel of the wagon.

"I have to rest awhile," the old man said and kneeled down beside Will.

He put his face in front of Will's, up close, and looked at him.

"I wish you could talk, young fellow," said the old man. "Tell me all about what happened. What they got you for and all."

"I can talk. Can't you hear good, old man?"

"Say," the old man said and leaned closer to Will. "Don't tell me they cut your tongue out."

He reached out to Will's chin and grabbed it and pulled it down until Will's mouth was opened wide.

"Nope," the old man said. "They didn't do that. Got your face cut up pretty bad, though."

The old man got to his feet and dragged Will to the back of the wagon. He put the upper half of Will's body on the wagon first and then he put up his legs. Afterwards, the old man got into the wagon and turned Will over until he was on his back.

"Well, we got this far," the old man said.

"Thanks, old man," Will said.

"Your eyes look like you understand me," the old man said. "I wish you could talk, though."

The old man reached in his pocket and took out a pocketknife. He kneeled down beside Will and reached for Will's arms.

"Hey, what you doing?" Will asked.

"Now, don't get scared," the old man said. "I'm not one of them. I'm just like you. Don't get scared. I'm just going to get you untied, here. Lord have mercy. They tied you up good."

"Hey, don't do that. Don't untie me," Will said. "I'll bleed more if you do that. It's a tourniquet. Don't take it off. Don't take it off."

The old man cut the twine first and then the tourniquet Will had made out of a piece of his shirt. The old man threw them out the wagon.

"There," said the old man. "You feel better now? You do? I know you do. I can see it in your eyes. Well, let's see if me and Bessie can get you to a doctor."

"Put the tourniquet back," Will said. "Put it back. Put it back."

The old man got to his feet and gave Will a half salute.

"You just lay here and take it easy, now. Lord have mercy. Wait till I tell Sarah about this," the old man said and went to the front of the wagon and sat down and started off.

Will was on his back looking up at the sky. It was blue now. He tried to raise his arms up and grab his shirt and tear it and make another tourniquet. His arms would not move. They were not there. He kept trying. He did not want to give it up. Then he thought of rolling over until his body was on his arms. Maybe that would help stop the blood, if the blood was coming. He tried to roll over. He couldn't roll over. He couldn't even roll his head over. The sky was still straight up and blue.

Will kept trying.

Back down the road the sun rushed toward the wagon and caught up with it and climbed up the back of it and up the soles of Will's shoes and down his legs and over his hands and over the pool of blood at his right wrist and up his arms to his neck and jumped over his head and rushed up the back of the old man and down the back of Bessie and made her ears perk up and then it rushed on up the road, heading west.

Appendix:
Selected Reviews

From *The New York Times Book Review,*
April 4, 1963

Set in a small Southern town, "If We Must Die" follows Will Harris, a Negro veteran of the Korean War, through a troubled day which begins with his attempt to register to vote, an act having more to do with pleasing his mother ("I'm so proud of you, son.") than with his own ambivalent convictions. He is denied the voting privilege on a "technicality," loses his job for daring to act as a citizen. He is later the victim of a violent assault by three varyingly moronic white brutes, an attempted castration that fails. Both the threat and the balk are oblique insights into Southern white desperation and impotence.

That is the bold shape of the story, but the drama hasn't the sound of its fury. Will Harris wants his girl to have "the good things in life" for "she deserved the very best" and in the intimacy of their aloneness he tells her, "Mary, I just want us to live like people. Real people." In a flashback to Korea, there is a touring Hollywood actress whose decency "made him feel like a human being. A real human being." While walking, Harris ruminates that, "People are sort of funny-acting things . . . they really are. But no matter how funny they act sometimes, most people are good-hearted, kind to others, and thoughtful."

If the platitudes were meant as narrative device, there is no subtle evidence of an undisclosed reserve, and the author's unwillingness to hover in the background diminishes the work. The book is in effect an extended prologue to a dramatic climax which has the mark of a good short story. Perhaps the episode originated that way (copyright dates noted are 1961, 1963). But whatever its origination, the closing scene, turning on a melancholy mishap and rendered with pathetic irony, is affecting.

From the very opening, the author's narration has a curious simplicity: it is almost as though the story were being told aloud in church, mindful of the children present—and even the savage setting in which a man is to be castrated evokes from no one, in utterance or thought, an invective more colloquial than "Aw, heck." The timorous language reflects the deeper flaw in this slim novel by a young Southern-born Negro who now lives in Westchester and works as an advertising copywriter. In limiting his vision to that of his inhibited hero, Mr. Edwards misses the masculine authority that might have given the violence an authentic sound. The threatened castration, therefore, which is ascribed to racism —an elemental source of it, surely—functions unwittingly as a symbol of a process already begun elsewhere, a vaguelly implied story the author conceals here.

Joseph Friedman

From *Herald Tribune Books*, August 11, 1963

"If We Must Die" confines itself primarily to one day in the life of a young Southern Negro veteran whose mother has prevailed upon him to exercise his rights by registering to vote. Mr. Edwards has a good eye for homely detail. With pedestrian deliberation, he shows us Will Harris waking up, eating breakfast, taking a final look at the Declaration of Independence, going to City Hall, then waiting around and finally being baited by two redneck clerks who have to hoke up a technicality to deny his rights.

Will Harris's act of courage sets off a chain reaction that nearly leads to his own annihilation in a ludicrously brutal act of vengeance by three more rednecks, but Will escapes and we are led to believe in the end that he will leave the South and try for a new life with his girl friend in another part of the country.

Junius Edwards is very good at dialogue, especially those tight-mouthed Hemingwayesque exchanges between the haters and the hated. He also seems to have a submerged awareness of the great resentments with

141

which the present generation of Negroes regard their elders.

But his manner is simply too pedestrian throughout. Aside from some momentary insights into what the boy and his girl friend want or into how and why the mother operates, it almost seems as if, in this first exercise in story telling, Edwards had deliberately avoided indulging in personalities. That is too bad because only by a truly intimate glimpse of individual Negro personalities can we come to understand the human harms which are an everyday occurrence in this country.

Richard Ellman

Reprinted from the *New York Herald Tribune Books Section*, August 11, 1963. Copyright © *New York Herald Tribune*.

From *Saturday Review*, August 3, 1963

Last spring I had a chance to hear and to see something of the Freedom Singers, a remarkable group of young people who sing the songs that have developed in the course of the struggle for civil rights as well as the older songs of the Negro people. But these are not only gifted singers; they are all field secretaries of the Student Nonviolent Coordinating Committee, veterans of many demonstrations, alumni of a variety of jails. To hear their stories is to be deeply moved.

The whole upsurge of the Negro people is something that might touch the imagination of any writer of fiction. There is not only the movement of the students—"those wonderful kids," as James Baldwin calls them. There is heroism of many kinds and on many levels, and of whites as well as Negroes. There are all sorts of conflicts, too, so that we have James Meredith in tears because of the rebuke of an NAACP leader. All around the fringes of the movement, and on both sides of the barricades, magnificent dramas are taking place.

Within the past few weeks three stories by eminent American writers have indicated some of the fictional possibilities. In *Partisan Review* Ralph Ellison's "It Always Breaks Out"—presumably a part of his forthcoming novel—takes off from a Negro jazzman's act of protest, the burning of his Cadillac on the lawn of an abusively anti-Negro Senator. The incident is discussed by a group of journalists, one of whom, a Southerner, undertakes to state what is political action on the part of a Negro. It turns out that everything a Negro does, from buying a bulldozer to joining the Book-of-theMonth Club, is political. The reporter's diatribe is high-pitched enough to be funny, but the point Ellison makes is serious.

In "Black Is My Favorite Color," published in *The Reporter*, Bernard Malamud looks at the general problem of the white person who is friendly to Negroes but, being white is, rejected by them. The narrator, Nat Lime, Jewish proprietor of a liquor store in Harlem, recounts a series of rejections, from the trivial to the serious. He says: "If they knew what was in my heart towards them, but how can you tell that to anybody nowadays. I've tried more than once but the language of the heart either is a dead language or else nobody understands it the way you speak it. Very few."

The most surprising of the three is Eudora Welty's "Where Is the Voice Coming From?" in *The New Yorker*, which is like nothing else she has written. Although it was published after the shooting of Medgar Evers, it must have been written before, and its relevance to that tragic event is uncanny. Here is a white man's story of how and, so far as he understands it, why he shot a Negro leader ("I done it for my own pure-D satisfaction.") It is a fiercely cold and powerful story.

The three stories in their widely differing ways show how much can be done with the subject of racial conflict, but of course the subject alone does not guarantee a fine story. How far achievement can fall below intention is illustrated by *If We Must Die*, a very short novel by Junius Edwards.

The plot can be quickly told. A young Southern Negro named Will Harris, a veteran of the Korean War, decides, partly because of his mother's urging, to register to vote. He goes to the courthouse, is kept waiting for a long time, is treated overbearingly by a pair of white officials, and finally is rejected on nonsensical grounds. That afternoon he is fired from his job, and discovers that he has been blacklisted everywhere in town. In the evening, after going to see his girl, he is waylaid by three whites, badly beaten, threatened with castration, and left to die.

That such things happen everyone knows, but that does not make the book credible. To begin with, Will is unbelievably naive. Although he is nervous about going to register, it does not seem to have occurred to him that there may be serious difficulties. One would suppose that any Negro in such a community would know of the experiences of other Negroes and would have a pretty good idea what to expect.

So far as the actions and words of the officials are concerned, the scene at the courthouse is well handled, but again we have almost no insight into Will's mind, though the story is told from his point of view. What he feels as the men taunt and badger him is left almost entirely to the reader's imagination. The same thing is true of the final scene: the kidnappers are plausible enough, but we are never made to feel what Will is feeling.

The style is curiously flat and unimaginative:

> When they reached the factory building, they went around to the back and went inside and downstairs to the toilet. They had their water cans down there. Each can was big enough to hold one gallon of water. They had to fill up those cans with water and take them up to the third floor with them where they worked so they could have water to drink when they got thirsty. The work was hard and it was hot and they got thirsty often. It took too much time to run down to the toilet every time they were thirsty. They weren't allowed to use the water fountain because it was for the other workers.

Nothing in the whole struggle for civil rights is more important than the attempt of Negroes to secure the vote, and yet Edwards has managed to make almost nothing of this theme in fictional terms. Clearly his heart is in the right place: he wants to protest against injustice and brutality. But, because he cannot bring his character to life, because he cannot make Will real to us, he leaves us quite unmoved.

It is interesting to note how much more each of the three short stories does than this novellette. Miss Welty tells us more about Southern whites who are inclined to violence. Ellison explores more deeply the nature of the conflict between whites and Negroes, Malamud shows us the predicament of the white man of good will. Of course, these three writers are experienced as well as highly gifted, and one cannot expect a beginner such as Edwards to equal their achievement, but one can ask for at least glimpses of imaginative power. Even as a piece of propaganda, the little book is ineffectual because it does not have the breath of life.

Granville Hicks

From *The Christian Century,* August 7, 1963

This novel, almost too well timed for this restless summer, is set in that section of the country where individuals from one group are often called "Boy"—and where "Boy" is now in a position to show resentment. A relevant nightmare of a book.